SAHARA

DESERT OF LOVE

**BY
MARIANGELA
DELFINO CAVERO**

" A writer is a world

trapped in a single person

Victor Hugo

ACKNOWLEDGMENTS

To God, who is always with me.

To my husband Aldo Cámere, for his unconditional support.

To my children Aldo Jr., Anita, Daniella, and Tyler, for encouraging me to keep writing.

Special thanks to my daughter-in-law Anita Cámere, who took the photo on the back cover.

To my beautiful and adorable granddaughters, Bianca and Alessa, who listen with such interest when I tell them my stories.

To Mr. Hamid Tagchloui, who gladly informed me about everything related to the desert, its customs, and its history.

PROLOGUE

This novel, inspired by and written in Sahara Desert, tells the story of Hassna, a little girl from an Arab-Berber family who is orphaned and given to her uncle, her father's brother, as her guardian and executor of her estate. Years later, she falls into a deep depression, and her uncle takes advantage of the situation, committing her to a mental institution. She tries to scape but is pursued by a hitman hired by uncle with orders to kill her.

It's a novel full of action, suspense, tragedy and love. The places that appear in the novel are real, as is the story of the European climbers of Mount Ilmil; Their names are fictional. This novel will keep you on the edge of your seat from beginning to end, culminating in an unexpected twist.

SAHARA DESERT OF LOVE

Malaga, Spain, one day in May, 9:30 in the morning.

Izza's cell phone rings several times. She rushes to answer it. In her haste, she trips over the edge of the bed. The cell phone is on her nightstand, she reaches for it and answers it agitatedly.

"I'm ready, Assim."

"Honey, we'll pick you up in five minutes. Did you talk to Latifa?"

"Everything's arranged, love. The driver will pick up Hassna from school and take her to Latifa's house until we get back. Omar will be happy to spend the afternoon with her playing video games." "I imagine these kids are inseparable.

We're here," Assim tells his wife.

I'll be right there," Izza replies.

The car pulls up in front of the house, and Izza runs out to meet her husband and get in the car.

"Salam aleikum, Mrs. Izza," the driver greets her.

"Alaikum assalam, Rashid." She greets the driver as he opens the car door for her.

"The company jet is waiting for us at the airport," Assim tells his wife, greeting her affectionately and admiring her beauty,"we'll arrive in Madrid before eleven in the morning, so it's a short half-hour flight."

"It's a beautiful morning for flying," Izza says to her husband. The sun's rays caress the day like the light of dawn, spreading across the horizon until the sun rises. I woke up full of optimism and energy. Aunt Amina will be happy to see me after so many months. Poor thing, she's so active and has a broken leg. I'll spend the afternoon with her while you go to the head office.

"The truth is that Fahim was planning to travel, but with the cold he has, it's better for him to stay home. Your partner is very weak, he's always sick, and his immune system must be very low."

Fahim, his partner and friend, owned a 30% stake in one of Assim's companies. They had been friends since their youth and remained very close, enjoying lovely family moments with wives and children, so that the children loved each other like siblings.

Malaga, 3:45 p.m.

Rashid went to pick up Hassna from school.

"Salam alaikum, girl," Rashid greets her.

"Alaikum assalam," Hassna replied.

The girl got into the car and sat down next to her school bag as they drove to Latifa and Fahim's house. The girl was eager to get to Omar's house.

It was a clear and cheerful day. They turned onto a wide avenue where leafy trees swayed rhythmically under a deep blue sky, the air crisp and the day bright. The vehicle took a turn and Hassna finally saw Omar's house with excitement. They parked the car and Hassna hurried out with deep joy to ring the doorbell. Omar came out to greet his friend and the children hugged warmly as they entered the house. Hassna greeted Latifa and she replied:

"How wonderful to see you home, dear Hassna! We will keep you company here until your parents return from Madrid tonight."

The children, very happy, went to the room where they found the video games.

3

"This time I'll win," said Omar.

"You always say that."

"We'll see; I'm thirteen years old, an eleven-year-old girl isn't going to beat me."

Assim Sabal Saadi belonged to an illustrious Moroccan-Arab family that owned numerous companies in Malaga, Granada, and branches in Madrid. He was married to Izza, of Berber and Arab origin, and had one daughter, Hassna.

They were a very happy family, despite the fact that his family opposed the marriage, as Izza did not come from a wealthy or high-born family. When he met her, Assim was dazzled by her beauty; those large almond-shaped eyes, dark and enigmatic as the night, captivated him instantly.

Much to the dismay of Assim's family, they got married. As the Wali did not give his consent, a judge married them. The groom's mother would have preferred a suitable marriage, and the groom's father would have asked to visit the bride's family to agree on the dowry with the girl's father, giving rise to the Hotoba (the first stage of the marriage proposal), where it was customary to read the first sura of the Koran, the Fatiha, and draw up the marriage certificate. Unfortunately, none of these ceremonies took place for obvious reasons.

After the wedding, Assim bought a beautiful house in the most elegant neighborhood of Malaga, where he settled. When little Hassna was born, her parents accepted Izza into the family, but they were unable to enjoy their granddaughter for long as they passed away a few years later due to their advanced age.

Madrid, 10 p.m.

The private jet took off for Malaga. It had been a productive afternoon for Assim at the board meeting. He seemed very pleased with the company's progress; he looked fondly at his beloved wife, who, in addition to being beautiful, had a sweet, warm voice that comforted him and gave him peace of mind even in difficult times.

Before visiting Aunt Amina, Izza had bought a nice birthday present for Hassna that her daughter would love.

"Honey, we'll be landing soon," said Assim, enjoying the clear, starry night sky that covered the trees with a silvery blanket.

"Woman, I can't wait to get home," Assim said, taking her hand affectionately. "It's been a very busy day. I'll be more relaxed once I'm home. Rashid will pick us up first, and then we'll go get Hassna."

She would have liked to stay overnight at Omar's house, but then who would wake her up for school tomorrow? They love each other very much; she says he is her best friend.

11:30 p.m.

The phone rings at Mr. Fahim Abdalah's house.

The employee answers, "Hello?"

"Good evening, this is a call for Mr. Abdalah."

"The gentleman is resting."

"It's urgent. The police are calling from the airport."

Latifa picked up the phone and answered the call.

"I am Fahim Abdalah's wife. He is sick in bed and cannot speak; he has lost his voice. What do you want?"

"Unfortunately, we are calling to inform you of a tragedy. Mr. Sabal's plane suffered a landing gear failure and crashed noisily onto the runway."

Latifa was paralyzed. Fahim, upon learning of the accident involving his partner and friend, got out of bed and hurriedly got dressed to go to the airport. But first he had to break the news to Hassna, who was waiting to be picked up to meet her parents.

Fahim and Latifa went to the playroom to break the news to the girl, which weighed heavier than a block of granite. They sat down, and Latifa with a sad smile hugged Hassna and told her the terrible news. Hassna was speechless. Her eyelids fluttered, her heart raced, her legs weakened, and she felt faint. She soon regained consciousness by breathing deeply as Latifa instructed her. Then she burst into tears with a pitiful cry. With a frightened face and a helpless look, she felt her body tremble and her thoughts rush through her mind, shaken by a cyclone of new emotions.

The sky clouded over without a moon and the stars fell into a pit of darkness, while her little being drowned in an avalanche of uncontrollable feelings. She felt a dark and intense fear explode as the rain hit the skylight again, revealing a sound of loneliness and sadness. Omar hugged his friend with anguish and announced:

"You are not alone, Hassna. This will be your new family. I promise I will always take care of you." Both children cried in each other's arms, merging their sadness of fear and pain.

"Hassna, stay with us tonight," he added. "Latifa, we'll prepare the guest room."

Latifa asked the employee to bring some lime blossom tea for the girl, who was struggling to convince herself that what was happening was not real. All of this had caused her inexplicable confusion, and her doubts tormented her as the hours passed with slow cruelty.

Fahim, alarmed by the news of the accident, went to the airport to see what he could do.

The ambulances from the hospital in Malaga arrived at midnight at full speed to transport the injured with possible severe burns, but there was nothing they could do: the bodies were charred, mixed with the rest of the plane, and there were no survivors. When Fahim arrived, they had just extinguished the fire. A large cloud of smoke spread across the horizon, the private jet looked like a shattered accordion, and the police and ambulances were quick to arrive at the scene. The charred bodies were in the custody of the medical examiner; no one was allowed to approach. Fahim simply watched and waited to be questioned.

After Monday night, there was a drastic change in Hassna's life. That night, she had no hope of falling asleep. The atmosphere was tense, the air in the house heavy. When she finally managed to fall asleep, she woke up drenched in sweat plunged into nightmares. Spent most of that hellish night awake, tossing and turning in bed occasionally falling back into a light sleep. She felt very insecure, alone in the world without her beloved parents; she would have preferred to die with them; she felt abandoned and let out a sob in the middle of the night.

Omar woke up to Hassna's crying. He went to the guest bedroom and whispered, "My dear friend." He hugged her with deep affection and sadness, holding her small body close in his arms. He felt Hassna's weak heartbeat, like that of a terrified bird. They both cried deeply.

He sat down beside her and looking at her friend, added: "I'll sleep at the foot of your bed, and keep you company every night, so you won't feel alone." Hassna agreed.

The night was long and painful, passing as slowly as a snail, until, amid faint hopes she fell asleep from exhaustion.

That night, Fahim called Assim's only brother, Manssur, who lived in Granada with his wife Lalla. He gave him the sad news. Upon hearing it, his heart sank and he immediately flew to Malaga. Manssur, a brother two years younger than Assim, was burly, tall, dark-skinned, with black curly hair, large dark eyes, a round face, a thick beard, and as solid as a brick.

As Assim was so busy, he rarely spoke to his brother. Unlike Assim, Manssur had devoted himself to gambling in recent years; his business was failing and he would soon go bankrupt. He had become bitter.

After Assim's death, the reading of the will declared Hassna the sole heir to her parents' vast fortune, leaving Manssur as executor of the estate until Hassna was mature enough to manage her inheritance. This meant moving Hassna to Granada to live with her aunt and uncle.

Nine days had passed and Hassna was still living in Latifa's house, finding comfort in her friend Omar, whose company eased her pain. The girl's residence was about to close and they explained to Hassna that she had to move to Granada to her aunt and uncles house. They were strangers to Hassna, as her father was very involved in his business and did not make time for family gatherings.

For Hassna, it was a very hard blow. First, she lost her parents, then she had to move to Granada, leaving behind her home, her memories, and, above all, her close friend Omar, whose name means prosperity in Arabic. They said goodbye with tears in their eyes and promised to talk, see each other, and spend time together every night on video calls until she fell asleep.

After the funeral and the novena for her parents, little Hassna left with her uncle to go home, collect her things, and take them to Granada to her new home at her uncle's house.

Her nanny, Jamila, had her luggage ready with a heavy heart. As Hassna walked through the interior of the large mansion, she sadly saw the furniture covered and protected from dust with white sheets. The girl moved slowly and silently, overwhelmed by loneliness and a deep anguish enveloped in a whirlwind of diffuse shadows, which gave the house a gloomy appearance. Everything she saw reminded her of episodes she had experienced with her parents. Her tender little girl's face was ashen and pale; sadness had swept away the last vestiges of her dreams. Everything was ready to close the house. With a tender hug, she said goodbye to her nanny, walking away with great uncertainty and nostalgia in her heart. As she left, the last light of dusk faded among the leafy sacred chestnut trees of Istán, a thousand-year-old specimen, where she used to play on sweet sunny mornings, saying goodbye to the little world she had forged over her few years.

They arrived in Granada at Uncle Manssur's beautiful house, located in the San Roque neighborhood, on the hill of Alicún de Ortega, the greenest and most elegant place in Alicún. Built in 1916, it was a neighborhood steeped in history and the most highly valued in the city.

Aunt Lalla came out to greet her, hugged her affectionately with a cautious and somewhat shy smile, and offered her condolences to Hassna and welcomed her to her new home. Lalla was very happy that the girl had come to brighten up the house and bring a wave of optimism. Hassna greeted her aunt shyly, her beautiful face wearing a sombre, pensive expression, which lit up momentarily when she felt the warm embrace of her aunt Lalla. They had been unable to have children. Every time she became pregnant, she lost the baby.

Lalla was a woman as beautiful as she was shy, without a will of her own, fearful of her domineering husband. She had no say in the matter, and he blamed her for not being able to give him an heir. She lived in her husband's shadow; they couldn't talk because he was always right. She endured his whims and mistreatment, rarely speaking so as not to upset him, and he always belittled some of her achievements.

Her beautiful face showed perpetual sadness, and she had not been seen smiling since she lost her last pregnancy due to her husband's psychological abuse. Lalla's married life was a daily catastrophe, full of sinister and perverse omens. Her husband had such influence over her that he owned her very words, constantly overwhelming her. No one had ever manipulated her as much as he did. He was a man with more twists and turns than a colonial curtain.

Many lovers passed through his bed, and when she reprimanded him, he denied it shamelessly. She suffered in silence. All she longed for was a quiet place to cry. She calmed her sorrows in the swamp of tears of sleepless nights counting stars and dreamy dunes, so as not to be consumed by the embers of a reckless man. Her life changed when Hassna arrived to cheer her up; the grand mansion became a hope for happiness for Lalla.

She led Hassna by the arm to see the room that had been reserved for her. They entered through the hallway where the tiles were covered with Turkish rugs of exquisite colors. Hassna's room was spacious and well-ventilated, overlooking the square, white courtyard adorned with red geraniums at the foot of the windows. The floor was decorated with Moorish-style tiles, and the walls and columns were covered with tiles adorned with white and blue designs. In the distance, the continuous murmur of water from a fountain in the center of that beautiful courtyard could be heard. But Lalla's happiness was short-lived. Manssur decided to send Hassna to a boarding school for girls at a prestigious school in Granada. She only came home on weekends to stay with her aunt and uncle.

Upon arriving at the boarding school, she befriended a girl of Berber origin named Rania, and they became very close. Eighty percent of Morocco's population was of Berber origin after intermarrying with Arabs who took refuge in the heights of the High Atlas Mountains.

Rania's parents were divorced and had remarried, and they kept the girl at the boarding school to ease their worries.

The two girls identified with each other. Both lacked love and family unity, and both craved attention. They attended the same classes, and played the same sports, and sleep in the same room. Hassna found in Rania the sister she never had.

Every night she would talk to Omar for a long time, and he would wait for her to fall asleep. Little by little, Hassna accepted this new way of life.

Hassna's twelfth birthday was approaching, and when she left school that weekend, Aunt Lalla had prepared a birthday cake decorated with an Aladdin's lamp on top and gave her the gift that Uncle Manssur had left for her to deliver as he was visiting his brothers' companies.

Hassna opened the small package and found a beautiful gold bracelet in the shape of a ring. She thanked him for the gift, put it on, and thought wistfully that it was her first birthday without her parents.

Rania arrived at the small celebration and Hassna spent it with her family and in good company.

Three years later:

Hassna had turned fifteen, was almost finished with high school, and her friendship with Rania was growing stronger. She had continued to talk to Omar every day since he arrived in Granada.

Omar, had just finished his first year at university where he was studying business administration. One weekend, he surprised

11

Hassna by showing up at Manssur's house. She was very happy to see him looking so tall and handsome; seeing him on video did not allow his to fully appreciate the change he had undergone as he did in person. Omar was also surprised at how beautiful her childhood friend had become.

"Let me see you, Hassna. Your name means 'beautiful' in Arabic, and it lives up to your pretty face."

Hassna had become a very beautiful girl. Her large, almond-shaped black eyes seemed even bigger now that her face was more defined. Her nose was fine and perfect. Her sensual mouth framed the elegance with which she wore the hijab or scarf, that covered her head and surrounded her neck. They hugged for a few minutes. He looked at her and couldn't believe how much his Hassna had changed.

They spent a lovely afternoon strolling through the Albaicín, one of the most famous areas of Granada.

Omar's father had a beautiful apartment in Granada, located on a hill overlooking the Alhambra, on Calle Elvira and Camino de Ronda, next to the Darro River, four hundred meters from the Cathedral of Granada. It was a Moorish and Andalusian neighborhood. He had the apartment with the intention of leaving it to Omar on his wedding day.

They headed to the Alhambra for a walk, as it was nearby.

They entered what was once a military zone and eventually became a royal residence in the mid-13th century, establishing the Nasrid Kingdom. Located on a very high rocky hill, its reddish walls gave rise to its name, the red castle or Alhambra in Arabic.

The midday sun was motionless, heralding a sweltering day. They strolled through the beautiful and artistic gardens, fountains, arches, and tiles with arabesque and Andalusian designs.

The gardens of paradise were a delight to their eyes: the tall, majestic columns carved at the top, the flowers and gardens typical of a palace, the row of perfectly pruned trees formed aligned columns, marking a beautiful green path.

They sat down on a bench, tired from climbing stairs and walking. There were few people around and they felt at home.

Omar took her hand, they looked at each other as if trying to guess each other's thoughts, she smiled with a look of surprise in her large, sombre eyes, thinking that in a few hours he would be leaving for Malaga.

The wood of the bench sighed with the midday mist embracing the beginning of love. Omar, looking at Hassna, said:

"You are very beautiful, Hassna."

She, feeling Omar's hand intertwined with hers, felt an unexpected tingling sensation and her heart skipped a beat. It was the first time she had felt that way about Omar; she had always seen him as an older brother, as her childhood playmate, and now that feeling that filled every fiber of her being was different, painting a world of fiery colors.

Was it perhaps love she felt? she wondered.

He looked at her again with great tenderness and took her hand once more. Hassna felt her heart beating fast and a shiver ran through her body; her skin burned and a drop of sweat slid down her back.

"Let's keep walking," she said nervously, as it was getting chilly.

They got up from the bench, Hassna adjusted her hijab, and they returned to the car, while the sun faded compassionately and a breeze stirred the branches of the trees, cooling the air. The gray light defied the sky, and little by little they were surprised by the rain that lashed the streets, and a curtain of rain closed in a short distance from the car. They took refuge under the roof of a room to wait for the rain to stop. Meanwhile, she let out a laugh like a free woman, and soaked, they hugged each other until the sun shone again in a clear sky.

"Let's go eat at the Palacio Andaluz!" Hassna exclaimed excitedly. "It's a nearby restaurant that serves Arab-Moroccan food."

They dried off a little in the car and headed to Plaza Almona in the Albaicín. They entered the restaurant and were kindly served by a Moroccan Arab. They sat in a quiet spot. The restaurant was somewhat hidden, but it seemed very cozy thanks to the exotic Moroccan decor, with golden and purple colors that exuded excessive luxury.

They ordered a vegetable tagine, which they ate with their right hand, according to Arab custom, and not with their left, as this is considered impure and is only used for hygiene.

They also ordered hummus, couscous, pasta, and finished with a Moorish tea.

Omar was very satisfied with the food, and Hassna was glad he liked the place. After eating, Omar paid the bill, and Hassna asked permission to go to the bathroom. Omar relaxed by smoking a shisha, or hookah, and the air filled with a cloud of vapor.

On the way home, Hassna encouraged Omar to play video games like in the old days.

"Let's see if you can beat me!" she challenged him.

The maid entered with a tray of Moroccan mint tea (borghi) in a small silver teapot and two small glasses. She poured the tea, holding the teapot slightly elevated so that the sound of the tea falling into the glasses could be heard. She placed them on the coffee table along with a couple of small bowls containing almonds, honey, and sesame cakes.

They settled down on soft cushions to drink tea, following the Muslim custom of hospitality.

They played for several hours, laughing as they reminisced about the days when Hassna lived in Malaga.

The time came to leave and say goodbye. Omar took her hands stroked her cheeks, gazed intently at her, and suggested they continue as a couple, since the ritual would be more formal when his parents went to ask uncle Manssur for her hand in marriage. Hassna accepted the idea without hesitation, trying to control the surge of emotions that overwhelmed her. She was happy that Omar was speaking with his parents to arrage the engagement. They said their goodbyes, and Hassna was so thrilled that her tired eyes instantly sparkled with happiness.

The next day, Hassna told Rania about Omar's surprise arrival and marriage proposal.

"You're crazy, Hassna!" exclaimed Rania, shocked by the news. "You're confusing romantic love with friendship. You've grown up almost like siblings. You're confused."

"Rania, I love Omar."

Rania was upset. Soon there would be an engagement, a wedding, and she would be left behind. Her friend would no longer be hers alone.

The following weekend, Rania suggested to Hassna that she ask uncle Manssur for permission to go to the Sambra del Monte.

15

"Aurora told me she had a great time at the flamingo cave; we're young and we have the right to live, Hassna."

"Rania, I think uncle Manssur will be out of Granada, so there won't be any problem with aunt Lalla's permission."

"Okay, friend! deal, enjoy life."

Hassna arrived home on Friday, greeted aunt Lalla, and asked her permission to go out with Rania and Aurora, her tutor.

"Where are you going?"

Hassna replied without hesitation:

"We're going to Sambra del Monte, in the Albaicín, to see a flamenco show. There's a minibus that will pick us up, take us there, and bring us back when the show is over."

"Hassna, you have my permission, but you're still too young to go out at night. Your uncle is very strict about going out, so I ask that you not come home too late."

"Thank you, auntie," Hassna replied. "I promise to come back as soon as the show is over. If you want, you can come with us. You never go anywhere. They say there will be lots of tourists and interesting people there."

"Thank you, niece, but I prefer to stay home. Maybe another time."

Hassna went to her room, lay down on her bed, and called Omar to tell him she was home and had permission to go out with Rania and her tutor to Sambra del Monte.

Omar responded kindly: "Be very careful on the street."

"Don't worry, honey, the bus will pick us up and then drop us off again. I can't wait for these two years to pass so we can get married and go out together."

"I talked to my parents about the engagement," Omar added, "they thought it was great news, they told me that when we were children, your parents and mine wanted us to get married."

"How my parents would have loved to attend our engagement and wedding," Hassna replied wistfully. "I promise you, my love, that I will be the most beautiful and happiest bride in all of Granada. I love you."

"And I love you too."

"I have to hang up, my love, see you tomorrow."

Hassna sat on the bed, crossed her legs in the lotus position, hugged the pillow, and rocked herself with a feeling of happiness, smiling tenderly.

Uncle Manssur spent his time traveling to supervise Hassna's businesses, which he managed and kept under control, but unfortunately he was addicted to gambling. He began to use funds from one of the heiress's companies to finance his vice, hoping to replenish them with a lucky win. This never happened. He spent his time billing fictitious expenses to have money to gamble.

As her uncle traveled a lot, he did not have time to supervise or control Hassna's education and discipline. In uncle Manssur's absence, it was easy for her to get permission from aunt Lalla.

Hassna felt sorry for her aunt and tried to make her happy. When she left school, she would invite Rania to her house and cheer Lalla up by combing her hair, fixing her up, and dressing her in her pretty clothes, which she never wore. They would try on different colors of hijabs and gold anklets on her feet, and when her aunt looked in the mirror, she would smile. She had beautiful hair, dark as tar, which contrasted with her large, beautiful topaz eyes, a tall, slender, elegant, stature, and a cocoa-colored complexion, but at forty, this beauty contrasted with her expression of distant anguish, taciturnity, and air of desolation. Then the girls would convince her to go out for ice cream or a walk downtown. There she was talkative and cheerful. The circumstances of her life with Massur had sown seeds of insecurity in her. Being with Hassna and Rania made her heart race like it did before she got married, enjoying her youth and forgetting her disdainful life.

Hassna's cell phone rang just as she finished talking to Omar. It was Rania.

"Are we going out tonight? Did they give you permission?" Rania asked.

"Yes, aunt Lalla spoils me a lot, she's very good to me, she reminds me of Mom."

"Then," said Rania, "we're ready to celebrate. Let's go out right now. See you at Plaza Nueva. From there, the van will pick us up and take us to the Albaicín."

They arrived on time; the small van was a few minutes late; it was still very early and there was no light. First, they stopped at the San Cristóbal viewpoint to admire the Alhambra; the street was full of curves and s harp turns. Together they watched the beautiful sunset, accompanied by a crowd of people who like them, were waiting for the moment to leave.

They returned to Plaza Larga, to the San Nicolás viewpoint, with a beautiful view of the city of Granada and the Alhambra. There were spontaneous musicians in that square. They continued on to the San Nicolás cistern, climbing steep slopes and cobbled streets, followed by bars and tapas, where many tourists gathered to enjoy the beautiful view of the Alhambra and the city of Granada.

As night fell, they sat down to wait for the van so they could leave on time for Sambra del Monte.

It was their first time attending a gypsy event. The place was packed with people. From outside, they could see the white walls of the facade covered with pots of red geraniums, which created a beautiful contrast with the white walls and gave it an Andalusian feel. They passed through a door with a small black iron arch and found several small tables with people eating tapas and drinking beer, waiting for the first show to end.

They sat down at one of the tables and ordered some tapas and three orange juices, then spent some time looking at the paintings and posters hanging inside. Within a few minutes, the cave emptied and everyone left very satisfied.

They went inside and sat on wooden chairs with straw seats, forming a large semicircle, leaving a large space in the center for the dancers. The walls were covered with paintings from all periods and photos of the dancers posing with famous people. The ceiling was covered with copper pots and plates hanging throughout the cave. Glasses of red and white wine were served to each spectator; they refused it, substituting orange juice instead, and the flamenco evening began.

Hassna, Rania, and Aurora were fascinated, watching the beautiful gypsy women sing, dance, and sway in their colorful costumes. Then a gypsy man entered the dance floor, stomping his feet with vigor and skill, experiencing and feeling the music that transported him back to his roots.

Satisfied with the performance and the atmosphere, they set off for home, but unfortunately uncle Manssur had arrived unexpectedly, pressuring aunt Lalla, as Hassna was not at home late at night.

"Where is the girl?" Manssur asked, his hypnotic eyes staring at Lalla with a gaze as sharp as a knife sliding between the gray light of the vertical wrinkles on his furrowed brow.

"I came home and remembered that Hassna doesn't go to school on weekends. Where is my niece?"

Aunt Lalla didn't know what to say or where to start.

In a broken voice, she replied:

"I let her go out with her friend Rania and her tutor to attend an event. She'll be here soon." She maintained the cold silence of fear.

"Very well," he replied with obvious euphoria, his expression skeptical and intimidating, as insensitive as a statue. Anger filled the air like a heavy breath of doom that made the hair stand on end.

She followed his every gesture with a fearful gaze, wondering what he would say to her, what he would do to her, in a chilling silence, and each minute passed with nightmarish slowness.

The clock struck ten at night, and luckily Hassna arrived and was surprised to see u ncle Manssur waiting for her at home with fiery eyes and a face sourer than a sack of lemons. Aunt Lalla's face was full of anguish, feeling submerged in the quicksand of her life.

Pale and emaciated like a dusty animal, he spoke, breathing deeply, the reddish color fading from his face:

"Is this the right time to arrive? A decent girl should stay at home, not show off in public places. Go to your room, we'll talk tomorrow."

"Okay, u ncle," Hassna replied humbly, heading to her room lost in dark thoughts, slipping discreetly into the darkness.

Mansur's tone of voice turned threatening toward Lalla, and her stomach filled with cold foam. With a malicious look and a hoarse voice, he rudely scolded her for letting his niece go, throwing recriminations in her face for the loss of her pregnancies, calling her useless for not procreating and raising a child.

Lalla felt belittled, hurt, and unhappy. Living with her husband was a perpetual agony, as his character became increasingly twisted with age. She looked out the window, hiding her eyes filled with tears of pain. The raindrops brought back memories of that bittersweet day that had broken her heart, and she felt alone again.

Hassna arrived at her room sad, upset, and worried about her uncle Manssur's attitude. She felt guilty for having embarrassed her poor aunt.

I can't wait to get married and live my life, Hassna thought, and get out of this house.

It didn't matter that Omar had three years left to finish his degree, she thought. She wasn't worried about the financial aspect; she would claim her inheritance and have enough money to cover her needs, and Omar could finish his studies and work in one of the companies.

They also had the house in Malaga and Omar's apartment in Granada to live in. Omar's family were honorable and wealthy people who loved her like a daughter. As friends of her parents, they had known her since she was a child and had always wanted the young couple to marry. Hassna went to bed that night like a restless turtle hiding inside its shell. During her hours of insomnia , she tossed and turned in bed, unable to sleep, suffocated by the folds of the sheets, her thoughts slipping out of bed and scattering across the floor like sand.

The fateful morning dawned with a beautiful bright sun in the immense blue sky, its light falling like golden dust between the curtains of her bedroom. Hassna woke up with a bad taste in her mouth, due to her encounter with her uncle the night before. Her face was marked by fatigue as she had barely slept all night and had spent it navigating the storm of her life. She got up quietly and went out to have breakfast. Uncle Manssur was smoking shisha, reclining on cushions in the beautiful Moroccan living room covered with colorful rugs and elegant tapestries.

Hassna approached him to apologize for what had happened. Uncle Manssur seemed restless and annoyed by her late arrival the night before and said to her with a smile as sharp as the edge of a knife:

"From now on, young lady, I will give you permission, and when I am away, you will not leave the house to go anywhere."

Hassna simply bowed her head and left the room, but she realized that aunt Lalla had not been seen for a long time and imagined the worst.

She spent a sad Sunday in her room. She waited for uncle Manssur to leave the house to visit aunt Lalla, who was in her room. She walked a few steps and stopped, knocked on the door, and asked.

"Auntie, may I come in?"

Lalla was lying down. Hassna entered and saw that she was wearing a veil that covered almost her entire fase. Like a lost soul emerging from the mud, she saw her exhausted face and the pillow damp from the stream of tears that had flowed from her onyx eyes. For Lalla, marriage weighed more heavily on her than her age. The curtain in the room was drawn, and the light of dawn illuminated half of her face, leaving the other half in shadow. Hassna was concerned because she only wore the hijab when she left the house or if there were any male visitors. Lalla looked at her for a few minutes with a gloomy sadness, thinking that her future was shrinking under the weight of her worries.

Lalla replied that she was not feeling well. Judging by her aunt's attitude, Hassna was sure that uncle Manssur had mistreated her.

"I'm so sorry about what happened last night, auntie," Hassna added. "It won't happen again."

Lalla lay in bed trying to survive, mired in a quagmire of humiliation. She was ashamed and worried about what her niece would think of the abuse she received from Manssur, unable to do anything about it. Hassna felt very sad that her uncle could treat Lalla this way, unlike her father who adored her mother and always respected her. She took the opportunity to say goodbye, hugging her affectionately as she was leaving early for school the next day.

She quickly left aunt Lalla's bedroom, fearing that uncle Manssur would return from the street. That day, Hassna spent the whole day in her room talking to Omar about what had happened, chatting until the first sounds of nightfall could be heard.

Uncle Manssur's oppressive control was impossible to bear and impossible to understand. The idea of returning home and finding herself alone, surrounded by the silence of four walls, was difficult for her. The tensions within her family during those days forced her to make decisions and resolve the situation.

Omar decided to meet with his parents to formalize his relationship with Hassna and celebrate the Hotoba ceremony (marriage proposal), in which the first sura of the Quran and the Fatiha are read, and the marriage certificate is drawn up. But first, Omar would have to arrange a visit with Hassna's family.

They considered the fall season, as it was the best month of the year to celebrate weddings. After discussing and planning it with his parents, Omar called Hassna to give her the good news. Hassna was very excited about Omar's news; she was looking forward to finishing school to start her new life. They spoke quickly and said goodbye, as she was at school and starting dance classes.

The girls got ready by choosing veils, essential accessories for a dancer that add a touch of ethereal fantasy to the dance.

They began with belly dancing, crossing the seven gates of the underworld, leaving a veil at each one to represent their soul so that they could belong in spirit to their love, representing in the veil the deepest and most hidden part of the female soul, interpreting sensuality, emotion, and mystery in dance.

Rania's group performed the candle dance, balancing a plate with candles on their heads, wearing a costume called Bedlah, exuding a mystical air as they moved their hips and legs with elegance and sensuality.

Next the belly dance moved gently, walking with the romanticism of veils, playing with different types of sensations and mystery, skill, intrigue, secrecy, and sensuality. Behind the veil, she performed slow, sensual rhythms expressing flirtation, creativity, and elegance, letting the veil fly gently as she danced barefoot.

Belly dancing originated in the sands where the sultan performed this dance in honor of the goddess of fertility. A slow rhythm, performed with a double veil.

Arab girls like Hassna learned from an early age to dance the Rags-baladi, a rural dance that harmonizes body and mind. She was an expert in almost all dances and from a very young age, she performed at home to the pride of her parents.

When the dance classes ended, Hassna excitedly told Rania about Omar's decision to ask her to marry him. Rania again advised her not to do it.

"That's not love! It's custom! You feel that with him you will be free, that's all, my friend." Hassna did not listen to her friend.

"It's decided, Rania. I'm not asking for your opinion, I'm telling you. We've already decided, and it's final."

Rania left the room mortified by her friend's decision, as the conversation had left her more tense than a cat with its fur standing on end.

Hassna had asked her teacher at school how, in Arab culture, one could opt to administer one's inheritance and how to assert o ne's coming of age. She discovered that these were the requirements: menstruation in women, nocturnal emissions (semen discharge) in men, the appearance of pubic hair, and reaching the age of fifteen.

"If you are an orphan, as is your case, Hassna," added the teacher, "your inheritance can be given to you if you are capable and mature enough to manage your assets, which have previously been managed by your guardian according to the Qur'an 4:6."

The problem was solved, which filled her with happiness and awakened in her a wave of hope that she would finally be free and could say goodbye to the suffocating and disastrous world in which she lived.

Months later.

When Hassna finished her studies at boarding school, u ncle Manssur was waiting for her at home, annoyed. He stared at her, his dark gaze sinking into the deep waters of her eyes to give her the news that Omar's father needed to set a date to visit the house and decide on the day of the Hotoba. Hassna was very happy, unlike her uncle, with the unexpected news, whose rough, dark curls had turned ash-colored. He began to retreat from the room like a poisoned tide.

Aunt Lalla was the most excited about Hassna's engagement, and they began to make preparations.

"My dear daughter, I wish you all the happiness that I cannot have with your uncle. I feel blessed that you will be able to leave, because otherwise you will be subjected to your uncle for the rest of your life. You are too young and beautiful to be locked up. I will miss you, my dear Hassna, but knowing that you are happy will make me very happy."

"Thank you, auntie, I will miss you too and will visit you when I can."

When the day arrived, Omar and his father Fahim arrived at Manssur's house, who greeted them and kissed them on the cheek.

"Salam Aleikum," Manssur greeted them.

They shook hands.

"Alaikum as-salaam," Fahim and Omar replied.

They entered the house and were served mint tea as a ritual of hospitality in three small glasses and two small plates with sweet sesame cakes, honey, and dates, which were placed on a table.

The dowry was set by Manssur, representing Hassna's father, and he gave his consent. Omar offered Hassna the diamond ring, performed the Hotoba (marriage proposal), the Fatiha, and drew up the marriage certificate.

Manssur prayed as usual. Hassna was beautifully dressed in a light-colored embroidered tunic and a matching hijab that covered her hair.

Omar and she couldn't stop looking at each other, gazing with love and hope. After the ceremony, Lalla offered a dinner that left the guests very satisfied. Then they said goodbye and left to return to Malaga.

Hassna and aunt Lalla thought about organizing everything necessary for the wedding. She would need seven dresses to change into as needed, and the last one was white. Takchita wore a Moroccan dress and carried a bouquet of flowers.

They planned to hold the wedding banquet in the gardens of ncle Manssur's house. After the wedding, they would go on their honeymoon and then move into the apartment that Omar's parents had given them in the Albaicín, as they had purchased it some time ago for Omar's wedding, and the apartment was very close to Hassna's aunt and uncle's house.

Uncle Manssur was very worried and upset about his niece's wedding, as he would no longer be in charge of managing the inheritance, which would pass into Hassna's hands. His company was bankrupt and he had huge gambling debts.

One week before the wedding.

They had reserved the mosque for the wedding and everything was ready for the banquet at Hassna's uncle's house. Omar spoke to Hassna and told her that he was going to have a bachelor party and that his friends would take him to the Turkish bath and then out to dinner. She confessed that she didn't feel like going and wasn't in the mood because she wasn't feeling well.

"It's just nerves, relax, honey, you'll be fine."

They talked until it was time for him to attend the event. Omar said an affectionate goodbye and went to shower and change clothes to meet his friends. The guys were waiting impatiently for him.

Rania called her to congratulate her on her engagement, even though she didn't agree with the wedding. Hassna asked her to be one of her bridesmaids, since she was her best friend, and she accepted.

Omar and his friends relaxed in the Turkish bath, but he felt a queasy sensation in his stomach that he thought was due to not having eaten anything all day.

Then they went to a Moroccan restaurant and ordered Arabic rice with chicken and almonds, tabbouleh, grape and cabbage rolls, couscous with lamb, and a vegetable tagine with peppers, eggplant, walnuts, almonds, and hazelnuts for the banquet. He tried a little of everything, as the food was meant to be shared.

When dinner was over, he just wanted to get home and take an antacid to calm his discomfort. He said goodbye to his friends and thanked them for the bachelor party.

He got in the car and drove home. He arrived anxiously, entered the hallway, trying not to make any noise, went to where his mother kept her medicines, and started looking for an antacid. The movement woke his mother.

"Son, do you need anything?"

"I'm looking for an antacid, Mom. I think the food didn't agree with me. My stomach hurts."

Latifa, his mother, couldn't find the antacid, so she prepared something to make him vomit what he had eaten. Omar took it and began to retch and vomit in the bathroom, emptying his stomach to the limit. However, the effort of retching affected his heart, causing a massive heart attack. He died on the bathroom floor in his mother's arms as she tried to revive him by hitting his chest.

She screamed, "Fahim! Call an ambulance! Omar is dying!"

She screamed in despair, "I killed my son!"

When the ambulance arrived, the boy had no pulse and his body was purple, so he was pronounced dead. The doctor certified the death certificate.

Fahim found himself in a whirlwind of thoughts. He didn't know where to start. He couldn't count on Latifa. She was out of control, suffering from an asthma attack. The ambulance gave her oxygen. Fahim was alone in his misfortune. He had to notify his family, especially Hassna.

When the ambulance left, Fahim began the ritual: bathing his deceased son as quickly as possible to free his soul from his body. This ritual could be performed at an Islamic funeral home, where the body was purified, but in this case, Fahim wanted to perform the ceremony for his son. The ritual included an odd number of baths with jujube leaves—five or more times, three, five, and seven—and a series of steps dictating which part of the body was washed and in what order.

First, he washed the right side during the ablution for prayer. Then he finished by anointing him with perfume. He did not receive visitors until the body was found wrapped. It was imperative that he be buried within three days of death. Then he dried and ceremoniously wrapped the body, covering it with three white cotton cloths, with a shroud or kafan, made of a special fabric. When the wooden box arrived, he placed his son inside without the lid and took him to the mosque.

At midnight, Manssur Sabal's phone rang. Lalla answered.

"This is Fahim. Is Manssur there?"

"He's sleeping," Lalla replied.

"It's an emergency; Omar is dead."

Lalla was speechless, unable to comprehend what could have happened to such a young boy. She hurriedly woke Manssur.

Fahim told him what had happened.

"I'm so sorry," Manssur replied, "we'll be in Malaga early tomorrow morning to accompany you."

"Tell Hassna."

"Shukran (thank you)," replied Manssur, deeply saddened.

"My wife has asthma and I'm here alone taking care of everything," added Fahim.

"I'm sorry, Fahim, we'll be with you soon.

Manssur hung up the phone and thought about breaking the bad news to Hassna at dawn, before leaving for Malaga.

First thing in the morning, his most difficult task was to break the news to his niece. The girl slept peacefully on her white satin sheets, her beautiful long silky black hair cascading over the pillow. Her face wore an expression of peace and tenderness that would soon turn to fear, terror, and despair. Aunt Lalla looked at her with pity, her dreams vanished, her beautiful wedding dress hanging waiting for the wedding day, her white veil and other accessories agonizing with sadness.

For a long time, she stood by the bed staring at her, not knowing where to start. Hassna, as if sensing the force of her aunt's gaze, woke up. She stretched, intrigued to know why her aunt was in her bedroom staring at her by her bed. Lalla approached her and said:

"When you're ready, we'll wait for you outside your room. Your uncle and I want to tell you something." Lalla left the room trembling with nerves and showing a pernicious discouragement.

Hassna, intrigued, quickly got dressed and left her room to have breakfast. Her aunt and uncle gathered their courage:

"Hassna, dear niece, I bring you bad news."

"What's wrong, uncle?"

Lalla hugged her while Manssur began to speak.

"Fahim called last night. Omar felt ill after returning from his bachelor party. He vomited so violently that he suffered a massive heart attack... and died. I'm so sorry, niece. We have to leave for Malaga as soon as possible."

Hassna was in shock.

"It can't be!" she replied, crying inconsolably. "I want to see him!" Hassna cried desperately.

Deep down, she didn't believe Omar was dead; maybe he was in the hospital fighting for his life.

"Omar can't do this to me! The wedding day is almost here! My fate can't be so cruel," she said to herself. Then she felt something preventing her from breathing and tightening her chest at the sad and terrifying news.

She sent a message to Rania, who showed up at the airport to accompany them on the sad journey.

Rania took her friend in her arms and hugged her affectionately and protectively. They traveled for an hour and a half until they reached Malaga.

During the flight, Hassna's heart was pounding and cold sweat ran down her body. As the minutes passed, anxiety, fear, and despair took hold of her, and she didn't know if she wanted to arrive soon or delay the trip. She was afraid to face reality, which she refused to accept.

It felt like a nightmare. For her, Rania played a very important role in her life. She was the sister she never had, the support of a mother and father who did not exist, and she gave her strength and courage. Despite being the same age, Rania was more mature and determined than Hassna.

They arrived in Malaga. As she got off the plane, Hassna felt her body losing strength and thought she was going to faint. Life had turned her world upside down, and she felt dizzy with grief and despair. Rania took her by the waist, and with sleepy eyes, they hugged and quickened their pace. They walked to the car that was waiting for them. Her self-control broke down, and she sank into an apathetic silence.

Early in the morning, the day dawned under a blanket of dark clouds. The family was at the mosque keeping vigil over Omar's body. Suddenly Hassna arrived dressed in white, along with Rania and her uncles. Widows used to wear that color for four months and ten days. She had not yet been married according to religious rites, but since the wedding was only a week away and the engagement had already been formalized, she felt she should dress that way as a sign of mourning. The service was brief, with songs, rituals, and recitations from the Quran. The women and men sat barefoot on the floor in separate areas, leaving their shoes by the door. The women, enveloped in a fateful silence, covered their heads and wore loose-fitting, modest dresses.

Hassna cried profusely in front of the box where Omar lay; that subtle love had vanished in an instant.

Before he was taken to the cemetery, Hassna, Latifa, and Rania gathered to say goodbye to Omar one last time. Hassna clung to the coffin and refused to let go. Rania took her by the arms and pulled her away, interrupting her thoughts. Pain invaded her body, a pain so intense that she could neither contain nor hide it. She wanted it to go away and for this nightmare, which was more like a horror, never to happen again.

The women remained praying in the mosque, only the men accompanied Omar to the cemetery.

At the cemetery, they took Omar out of the coffin and placed him on the ground, putting his body in contact with the earth. The body was placed on its right side facing Mecca. The grave had only a flat tombstone with inscriptions in Arabic. The first sura of the Quran was read, followed by prayers. Those in attendance threw handfuls of earth onto the grave and prayed humbly to Allah for the deceased.

Hassna wanted to stay at her home in Malaga with Rania, as according to the rules of the Quran, the grave was visited on the third and ninth days and on the fortieth day, as they had to recite the Quran for three nights, according to the teachings of the Prophet Muhammad, the Quran, and the Sunnah.

Some friends of the bereaved brought them food so that they would not have to worry about such details, and after the funeral, they brought them flowers. They offered their condolences briefly and respectfully, and then went home.

The dark path of her life began when everything was smiling at her, her suffering was gentle and resigned, and her torture was cruel and merciless. She felt out of place in her own home, like a ghost in someone else's house from one day to the next. Embraced by her friend Rania, they entered the house.

Hassna, filled with pain, sobbed, "My pain will always remind me of this love that is gone forever, whose traces I may never find again." She felt alone and wandered aimlessly through the immense house covered with stretched canvases.

33

Her upbringing had been rigid and cold in the shadow of her uncle's mansion. She cherished a dream with Omar that actually evaporated with the sudden swiftness of the wind when he said goodbye. She was left with the imprint of a lost love in the tragic sublimity of a bachelor party night.

The next morning, the morning sun woke her up beside him. Hassna, realizing that it had not been a nightmare, returned to her terrible reality, cried again like a child, and incongruous thoughts ran through her mind. She regretted waking up; while she slept, she had ignored all misfortunes and found peace.

Hassna walked th rough the rooms of the house, which were covered with cloths to protect them from dust. She uncovered them and sat down on some soft cushions. Jamila, the lifelong housekeeper, upon learning of the tragedy Hassna was experiencing, moved back into the house to take care of her.

She brought them a tray with mint tea and the usual honey and sesame cakes. That day, Hassna did not leave the house and spent her time wandering through the rooms flooded with orange light that shone and then faded. She went to the terrace lit by the morning sun and sat in an armchair where the sun shone behind her. She wiped her eyes, which were clogged with the dry and wet tears that had accumulated during the night. Her heart was weary, her body exhausted by suffering, and finally, she let out a cry of pain. The trees groaned and swayed as they watched her, and the blinding sun hid behind the clouds sweeping across the sky.

"I raise my arms to the sky, but no matter how hard I try, I can't reach you. Are the clouds blocking my view? Where are you, my love?" Hassna burst into tears.

Rania went to look for her.

"I've been looking all over the house for you, Hassna. What are you doing here alone and sad?"

"Thinking, dear Rania, thinking."

That night, Hassna went to bed early. She was exhausted and tired, and fell asleep instantly. She saw Omar's face in her dreams and her heart sank. She woke up screaming and sat up in bed, sweaty. Rania heard her, went into Hassna's room, hugged her, and sat at the foot of the bed with her.

Hassna and Rania returned to Latifa's house the next day to pray. Omar's mother told her that her son had died of congenital coronary anomalies, a genetic disease. He had suffered an acute myocardial infarction. It could have been due to hereditary factors of heart disease, high blood cholesterol levels, stress, or anxiety, aggravated by the force of his retching. They couldn't believe it: a boy in his twenties had died of a heart attack.

Hassna asked Latifa to talk to Fahim about transferring Omar's body to their home to bury him in the garden.

Latifa couldn't believe what she was hearing.

"Hassna, you know very well that the law of Allah, our religion, does not allow the deceased to be moved to another place; they must remain where they are, and I tell you that Fahim will never allow it."

Hassna was not satisfied with Latifa's response. When she returned home, she went out into the garden in search of a suitable place to carry out her task. Whatever happened, she wanted to carry out this macabre project. Rania saw her looking for something in her garden and asked her:

"What are you looking for?"

Hassna told her what she wanted to do.

"Rania, you have to help me with Jamila. Between the three of us, we can do it. I can pay someone to help us move it. We'll do it at night."

Rania's hair stood on end when she heard such nonsense; her eyebrows rose toward her bangs like frightened birds, with the force of a gale, and she did not approve of such madness.

"I won't help you desecrate a grave. Get that idea out of your head; we'll end up in jail and on trial for violating a grave. Let's go back to Granada where you have your aunt and uncle and me. In this house, you'll be alone with sad memories behind anonymous walls. Let's go back, my friend," added Rania, hugging her affectionately.

Hassna thought for a moment and agreed. They said goodbye to Jamila in tears, and she locked the house again.

They arrived in Granada and Hassna felt sad and melancholic, thinking: "How much I have traveled within myself during these years of tender loneliness. I have already lost the only thing I had left: Omar. I cannot even mourn his loss at his lonely grave, because even that has been taken from me."

Sadly, she relived the fallacy of her own life in a ghostly memory. She fantasized that perhaps he would return from the dead one day, without warning. This memory kept her alive with the hope of the promise he had made to her, that he would always be with her. And yet she could not satisfy her own dreams. She remained tied to the nostalgia of her happy childhood and adolescence. Aunt Lalla suggested that she see a doctor to treat the depression she was suffering from due to her grief.

When Manssur found out, he found the solution to her problems. Cunningly, Hassna was admitted to a psychiatric clinic. A doctor friend advised him that, in exchange for a large sum of money, he should have her committed as insane.

Hassna's aunt did not know that Manssur had embezzled funds from one of Hassna's companies, nor did she know of his evil intentions towards her niece. To preserve his fortune, he declared her insane and incapable of managing her assets and left her in the sanatorium for life.

A month and a half had passed and Rania had heard nothing from her friend or anyone else who could provide her with information. She was told that, on the doctor's orders, Hassna could not receive visitors. Rania began to suspect that something very strange was going on: why couldn't her friend receive visitors and why was she in a psychiatric clinic if all she was suffering from was depression?

Aunt Lalla knew nothing about it and was also worried. Rania asked her to find out the address of the clinic so she could go and see her.

Since it was impossible to talk to Manssur, Lalla waited until he left on a trip to search through the papers in his study. The desk drawer was locked. Looking through several cards that Manssur had stacked in his card holder, she began to sort them and found the name of the mental hospital.

Rania did not sleep that night; she tossed and turned in bed until she came up with a plan to get Hassna out of that place.

Lalla and Rania headed in that direction on the outskirts of the city at night. It was a dark and windy night; the trees cast ghostly shadows, the wind whistled, and anxiety invaded Rania's body. After a couple of hours of driving, they found the right place. It was quite remote and deserted, with many trees surrounding the ranch and lots of vegetation camouflaging the psychiatric clinic. She parked near the compound; it was a very large, two-story white house surrounded by tall black fences and large gardens. Rania got out of the car, leaving Lalla waiting in case she had to leave quickly.

She walked a short distance, quietly entering the property, hiding behind tall, bushy cypress trees, and saw a nurse leaving.

Rania picked up a rock and knocked her out with a blow to the head. She hid her body by dragging it behind a bush. Then she stripped her and put on her uniform, used the duct tape she had brought with her to gag her, and tied her hands and feet to the bush. When she had everything under control, she entered through the front door pretending to be the nurse.

She walked down long, cold corridors lit by dim light, asked a nurse how to get to a patient's room, and was told where to find the records. As it was dinner time, the corridors were quiet and the place was cold. It was easy to find the records and find out where her friend was. Then she headed to where Hassna was. On the way, she ran into another nurse near the bathroom, knocked her down with a single blow, and dragged her into the bathroom. She stripped her naked, gagged her with duct tape, and locked her in the toilet seat. Rania slipped behind the door, taking her clothes and shoes with her, in case she had to leave with Hassna.

Rania, acting completely natural, without moving a single muscle in her face, entered the room and approached Hassna, who was lying there looking drugged and staring into space.

"Hassna, Hassna, wake up." Rania gently shook her friend. "It's me, Rania, I've come for you, my friend."

Hassna looked at her, coming out of her stupor, opened her eyes in surprise, and gasped.

"Get me out of here! They'll be here soon to give me my medicine!"

"Don't take it, throw it away," added Rania.

Minutes later, they heard the door open and Rania quickly hid behind a piece of furniture. Hassna pretended to be asleep; it was time to administer the sedatives. The nurse shook her to wake her up. Hassna pretended to take them and closed her eyes as if she were falling asleep.

"Very good," said the nurse, after taking her blood pressure and pulse. "You've behaved better today. You know that if you don't cooperate, cold water jets and electric shocks will make you see reason, so if you behave yourself, you won't have to undergo those treatments in a straitjacket." She wrote down the results of the various treatments on the chart and left.

Hearing this, Rania felt guilty for not having found a solution in time to prevent Hassna from being admitted to a sanatorium.

Listening to the nurse, Rania couldn't imagine how much her friend had suffered during her confinement. Rania came out of her hiding place. Hassna took the medicine out of her mouth. Her friend dressed her in the nurse's uniform; the shoes were a little small, but she managed to put them on. She combed her hair and covered it with the nurse's hijab.

Hassna was afraid of being caught and locked up again in the punishment room.

"Rania, my dear friend," Hassna said, "I had already lost hope of fighting. I even agreed to take the drugs that only made me sleep. After all, I didn't care about living."

"Don't say that, Hassna; I'll get you out of here."

"But how are we going to get out?"

"You'll have to recover, walk around a bit before we leave. We'll both walk out the exit door chatting, with our purses, and you carrying this notebook. Are you okay?"

39

"I'm a little dizzy, but I'm fine. Come on, let's not waste any time."

They walked calmly toward the exit door. Suddenly, a deep male voice said:

"Ladies..."

The two women stood still, motionless. Rania turned her head, while Hassna broke out in a cold sweat from fear, but she didn't let herself be overcome by the panic that was invading her. She took a deep breath, but inside she was overcome by a strong attack of anxiety.

"Can you tell me the time, please?" asked the man.

Hassna took a breath and the anxiety disappeared.

Rania replied, "It's nine o'clock at night."

"Thank you," said the man.

They walked naturally and arrived at the place where the car was waiting with aunt Lalla.

"Where are we going?" Hassna asked.

"To my house," replied Rania, "you'll be safe there."

Aunt Lalla hugged her and noticed that she was thin and haggard, with large dark circles under her eyes.

When they told Lalla where Manssur had taken her and everything her poor niece had suffered, she was enraged by the incident and offered them all her help.

"Don't worry, I don't know anything, I'll keep quiet as the grave."

Lalla left the two girls safe at Rania's house and headed home.

At home, Rania offered her friend mint tea and honey and sesame cookies. They drank tea sitting on colorful cushions and beautiful soft rugs that covered their feet.

"They won't look for you here yet."

"But what am I going to do now?" Hassna asked her friend.

"You have to leave Spain first thing tomorrow morning."

"Without clothes? Without a passport or money, I won't get anywhere."

"Hassna, you're my size. I'll give you clothes and a small suitcase with the essentials, as well as enough money (dirhams) and my passport. Starting tomorrow, you'll be Rania Nazer. With the veil, no one will notice. We look very similar; people even mistake us for sisters."

"Where will I go?"

"Somewhere where no one can find you: the Merzouga desert in Morocco, North Africa. Don't worry, shortly after you leave, I'll apply for a new passport and say I lost it, and we'll meet up."

"Thank you, Rania." They hugged each other affectionately.

"I'll always be with you when you need me, Hassna, and I'll protect you."

"You're a good friend, Rania."

Early in the morning, Rania, in collusion with Aurora, her tutor and lady-in-waiting, who was authorized by Rania's father to grant permissions and trips, took Hassna to the first flight to Tangier. Hassna went through immigration, presented her passport, and tried to hide her nervousness. They stamped her passport, and she went through customs, relaxing her tense body. As she headed to wait for her flight, she sent a text message to Rania with an "OK."

In the small suitcase, Rania had packed a black burqa for her to wear in Tangier. Hassna had traveled to Morocco as a child, when her maternal grandparents were still alive. She spoke English, Arabic, Berber, and a little Barilla. The Berber language, called Amazigh, which means "free man," has at least 300 dialects.

She remembered her mother telling her that Berber traders were responsible for bringing goods from beyond the Sahara to the cities of North Africa. Her mother's family, who were farmers in the valleys and mountains, were sedentary; in ancient times, they were nomadic indigenous peoples settled in North Africa. Farmers belonged to the lower class, and the upper class belonged to the merchants.

"Who would have thought I would come to the place where my mother lived," Hassna thought.

The plane was not full; luckily, no one was sitting next to her. Shortly before landing, she saw green fields and hills forming a mirage in the distance from the plane. Vast forests climbed the mountain slopes, opening up to valleys where flocks of sheep and houses could be seen in the distance, illuminated by the amber twilight.

As he approached the airport, he saw mountains dotted with houses and wild palm trees, hangars, and a row of closed offices or warehouses. The weather seemed sunny and a little windy, judging by the gentle swaying of the palm leaves. He saw countless yellow flowers populating the fields.

They landed in Tangier at Batouta International Airport. Once again, he went through immigration and customs and finally exited. He went to an office and rented a 4x4 SUV in the name of Rania

Nazer for three months, showing his passport and information and paying 400 dirhams per day.

He sent Rania a text message and wrote, "Everything went well. I miss you."

She grabbed a map and ventured across the Berber Arab lands, the place of her ancestors and which her mother longed for so much. It would be a long journey to reach the desert. Along the way, she passed countless yellow wildflowers and remembered seeing them from the plane, as well as herds of sheep and cows among the hills.

Granada, the night before.

There was a great commotion at the psychiatric hospital when two nurses were found almost naked and gagged, one in the bathroom and the other outside. They had been assaulted with a blow to the head, and a patient was missing. The security camera was not working, and it was not possible to determine how the attack, kidnapping, and escape had occurred.

The alarm was raised in all the wards.

"If the girl is inside the compound, we'll catch her easily."

The alarm was heard everywhere. Uncle Manssur's doctor friend wanted to search the inside of the building first before notifying Hassna's uncle.

"She can't have gotten very far. Let's not alarm Mr. Sabal. If we don't find her, we'll call at dawn, unless someone has helped her escape."

First thing in the morning, Manssur was called to be told of his niece's escape.

"What do you mean she's not there?!" Manssur shouted furiously, spitting fire like a dragon. "Such an expensive place and they don't have security! Search under every rock and find her!"

"She couldn't have escaped on her own, Mr. Sabal. Someone helped her, but who? We're investigating who could be behind this."

Manssur hung up the phone in a rage. He had hired a trusted private detective and a hitman to find the girl. "I want her dead or alive. Here's her photo."

Manssur arrived home and called Lalla.

"Do you know that Hassna has escaped from the hospital?"

"When? How?" asked Lalla.

"Last night."

"I didn't know anything," Lalla replied.

Lalla felt in control of herself for the first time, helping to free Hassna.

When Manssur entered his office with the stealth of a snake, examining even the most imperceptible details, he realized that his things had been moved. Suspecting that Lalla had participated in the escape, he called her again and asked, "Who has been snooping through my things?"

She replied that she knew nothing, that no one had entered the office, or that perhaps the maid had moved something while cleaning. Manssur, furious, grabbed her by the neck and squeezed. Lalla revealed nothing. Manssur did not believe her and locked her in the bedroom, taking her asthma inhaler and cell phone with him. Anger burned and glowed in his eyes, his expression sullen. He walked away muttering, his steps firm and hurried, while the fight dragged on with difficulty and without success.

44

"Now we'll see if you talk," he said.

Manssur got the address of Rania's house, as she was Hassna's best friend, and hired a second detective to watch the house, thinking that perhaps the girl was hiding his niece there.

He called Fahim's house in Malaga to see if they knew anything about her, but everything was negative. He even sent someone to look for her at the closed house that had belonged to her parents. Hassna had disappeared.

He searched her house for her documents: passport, driver's license, bank account, all the paperwork was intact and in place, as was her credit card. In short, everything was in its place. It was a mystery where she could be without money, without documents, and without clothes.

After three days of searching, he reported the case to the police, but the search was in vain. Hassna's photo was published in the press as a missing girl, and a reward was offered for any information on the whereabouts of the mentally ill girl who had escaped from a psychiatric hospital and was dangerous.

The escape

When Hassna entered the city of Tangier, the fourth largest commercial city, she felt the magic of this exotic land situated between two seas, the Atlantic and the Mediterranean, and between two continents, Europe and Africa. She felt at home in this place of diverse cultures: Arab, Muslim, Jewish, and Christian, cultures that maintained their customs without mixing.

She parked her vehicle and entered the medina, surrounded by countless shops selling crafts, food, spices, and clothing. There she found an oasis of absolute freedom, mingling with the people, perceiving the burning fragrances of incense, sneezing from the variety of spices she breathed in, saturating her lungs. As she couldn't find what she needed to continue her journey, she quickly returned to the truck, dodging the merchants and the large crowd of vendors who followed her and offered her their products, insistently lowering their prices.

She passed by the port, breathing in the healthy, warm, fragrant breeze, with the sun sinking into the sea and tinging the clouds with a pale pink, while seagulls flew over the blue horizon. She stopped to gaze at the sea next to a small fishing village. She was hungry and headed to the Hafa Café, near the Marshan neighborhood in the city's bay, where terraces with steps offered a spectacular view of the Strait of Gibraltar.

She got out of the truck and went into the café, bought food to go, and ate as she walked (batbout), Moroccan bread that her mother made with semolina and wheat flour, similar to pita bread. But she made it in a frying pan and liked to eat it with sweet and savory ingredients.

Hassna bought white cheese, honey, and nuts so she wouldn't have to stop to eat and could reach her destination as soon as possible. She passed by the beach at sunset and appreciated the beautiful reddish color of the sunset. She continued her journey feeling fear and nostalgia. She felt safe wearing the burqa, although driving in it was a little uncomfortable and the sweat made her itch more than a wool blanket. With it on, she could only see; the rest of her body was completely covered. Wearing it was relentless in the scorching African climate. The heat overwhelmed her and she succumbed to exhaustion, floating internally in a pool of sweat.

She looked at the map to see how far Tetouan, called the White Dove, was: one hour and fifty-six minutes.

She was driving on a well-maintained road, the journey was entertaining and picturesque, there wasn't much traffic, and from time to time she passed trucks carrying goats to be sold in the souk or goods bound for the medina.

He entered the White City, reached Mohamed V Street, and then Hassan II Square, where she stopped in front of the Royal Palace. she admired its walls and beautiful Moorish and Spanish-style gardens. The weather was warm and dry, and soft light filtered through the hellish summer haze. He passed a group of women wearing burqas, either to protect themselves from men as if they were an unworthy contagion or to cover their faces with a scarf that clouded their senses in the heat.

She felt the need to enter a mosque and parked the van. Outside the medina, she found quaint shops of artisans, jewelers, and silversmiths blocking her path and offering their wares to everyone who passed by. Hassna shook her head hastily.

She entered Terrafin Street, covered by wooden arches, and then continued walking through the labyrinthine medina, with its picturesque stalls selling dried fruits, colorful spices, clothes, and scarves. She encountered people passing by in their carts pulled by donkeys and passed several grocery stores, jewelry stores, bakeries, and restaurants outside the market.

Finally, she entered the mosque to give thanks to Allah and ask for his protection. As a Muslim, she prayed five times a day facing Mecca and fasted during the ninth month of the lunar calendar. The mosque was beautifully decorated with Moorish tiles on the floor and large columns.

Hassna left the mosque, her gaze lost in the crowd, and returned to the van parked in front of Hassan II Square, which connected old Tetouan with the new city. From there, she headed to the "Riad Blanco," which had a large sign that read "Moroccan Food." She decided not to go out to eat so as not to waste time, but when she saw the place where they sold pastries and cakes, she couldn't resist getting out of the vehicle to buy some buns to eat on the way.

She hurried along the south coast, passing the most beautiful and charming beach in Morocco. It was 61 kilometers away, a 57-minute drive. She was tired, tense, uncomfortable in her burqa, and drenched in sweat. She wasn't used to wearing it, but it was the only way to go unnoticed, to feel protected and free to walk anywhere without being recognized.

She ate on the way, as her nerves had whetted her appetite. She was looking forward to arriving and spending the night in a typical Moroccan riad.

She continued on to Chefchaouen, the blue city, so named for its streets lined with blue and white houses, beautifully decorated with countless pots of colorful flowers that filled her soul with peace and joy. The Jewish exiles who fled Spain during the Reconquista and settled in Morocco, operating as a business, monopolized the salt industry once they settled there.

The afternoon was dark. Hassna stopped on the side of the road and sent a text message to her friend Rania.

"I'm fine, I've arrived in Chefchaouen, I'm looking for a riad to stay in, I'm very tired. How are things in Granada? I miss you."

Rania replied to the message.

"I'm so glad you're okay. I don't want to scare you or make you nervous, but your uncle Manssur has hired a private detective to watch me. Yesterday I realized he was following me. He probably thinks I'm hiding you at home. The worst thing is that he has reported you to the police as a crazy woman who has escaped from a psychiatric hospital. Your photo is in all the newspapers in Spain; I'm afraid some of them might end up in Morocco. Be very careful and don't expose yourself. I wish you luck and I'll keep you informed. I miss you too."

Hassna was very worried. She tried to find a riad, but it was getting dark, the full moon had already risen over the quiet streets of Chefchaouen, and she just wanted to get there and rest anywhere.

She spotted a large white house with blue doors and a tiled roof, "Riad Jamila." It looked like a quiet and clean place. She entered the lobby, where a young woman was behind the counter.

"Salam aleikum," Hassna greeted her.

"Aleikum Salam," replied the girl.

"I need a single room."

She registered as Rania Nazer.

"I'll only be staying tonight," Hassna added.

"Go straight ahead, enter the large square courtyard with a central fountain. Around it you will find the dining room and other areas branching off from the common areas, living rooms, and bedrooms. The young man will guide you."

Hassna admired the place. It had two floors with multiple arches decorated with Moroccan-style blue mosaics, as well as wooden railings combined with black wrought iron bars.

They arrived at the room. Hassna went into her bedroom and the boy left her suitcase on a chair.

"Shukran," Hassna thanked him and gave him a tip of five dirhams.

She locked the door, took off her burqa, and lay down on the bed. She closed her eyes for a few minutes, stopping her rumination on her sorrows, displaying a thoughtful and relaxed stillness.

Then she took a bath, looked at her gaunt face in the mirror, changed her clothes, took a tunic and a hijab out of her suitcase, put them on, and went to the dining room, decorated with authentic Moroccan originality.

She was the only one in the dining room as it was late. She was served mint tea and the usual honey and sesame cookies.

"Shukran," Hassna thanked them for the welcome gesture.

Then she ordered couscous with vegetables and fig semolina for dinner. She was very satisfied, as she had been living on pasta and cakes since she left Granada. She retired to her bedroom, went to bed , and the next day began her journey to Fez. That night she slept exhausted from the trip, lost in her own shadows.

Dawn broke with light filtering through the crack in the window. She sat up and went out onto the terrace of her bedroom. She stretched her still-sleepy body and, as she did so, admired the beautiful mountains, serene and immobile witnesses to centuries of existence, bathed in the mauve light filtering through the horizon. The silent peace and clear blue sky immediately relaxed her and loosened her tense muscles.

Admiring the beautiful morning, she thought about making the most of it by putting aside the burden of sorrow she had been carrying for so long. Forgetfulness crep tinto her life like a mist; now she had to worry about something real and important: saving her life. She went into her bedroom, got dressed, put her headscarf on, and went down to the dining room with her suitcase.

The Moroccan breakfast consisted of crumb-free bread, freshly squeezed orange juice, fruit, honey, cheese, and dates. Hassna

50

helped herself to everything and ate it, as she had several hours of driving ahead of her. After breakfast, she left the Riad Jamila and set off for Fez. Along the way, she saw argan groves lining the road, and she was also struck by the countless goats of all sizes perched in the trees to eat. Seeing this unusual scene, she stopped the van. A Berber girl approached him and brought him a baby goat to pet and take a picture with. However, given the circumstances, he declined the photo. Hassna gave her a tip, petted the little animal, and continued on his way.

She skirted the forests of the Rif, passing by the Roman ruins of the city of Volubilis and its picturesque villages until he reached Meknes.

The journey seemed long, but the road was in good condition and from time to time, trucks, carts, and donkeys pulling carts passed by.

Finally, she arrived in Fez, the intellectual city of the kingdom. She headed for the labyrinthine medina with its wide walls protecting the city of nine thousand four hundred streets. Fourteen kilometers of ochre-colored walls, a stimulus for the senses with its narrow streets, corners, and shaded alleys. He headed for the tanneries in search of a small bag, passing countless pools side by side, used to process and dye hides that gave off a foul odor.

She quickly climbed to the second floor and found countless suitcases for sale: clothes, rugs, bags, and shoes made of brightly dyed lambskin. She bought a small bag and returned to the truck.

She passed by the madrasa and was impressed by its mosaic-covered walls and beautifully carved doors, which displayed art representative of Moorish, Andalusian, Jewish, and Berber culture.

She remembered her mother telling her that Fez had 185 mosques, the grandest of which was Karaouine. She would have liked to stop and pray, but she wanted to reach her destination as soon as possible.

Before leaving, she filled up her gas tank, using her precious purse for the first time, and paid seven hundred and twenty dirhams. The trip was supposed to take three hours and twenty-nine minutes. She passed numerous cobblestone streets and Moorish domes, and hug e houses in residential neighborhoods. She left early to arrive on time, as there was little lighting at night and a high risk of drug trafficking and police car searches. She was very tired and tense from the trip, so she stopped at a café, drank mint tea, and bought some buns, figs, and sesame and honey sweets for the road.

From Fez, she continued through the Middle Atlas, where green embraced the mountains and beautiful cedar fields; the road wound along a winding serpentine. She looked at her watch and saw that she had one hour and nine minutes left. She continued her journey and finally arrived in Ifane, a picturesque place known as the Switzerland of Africa for its gabled architecture, typical of European countries, where the roofs of the houses peeked timidly above the trees. All along the way, she remembered her mother's conversations in which she longed for her homeland.

Granada

Aunt Lalla was locked in her bedroom. Manssur went to the kitchen and ordered the maid to go shopping at the market.

Lalla was exhausted in her room, her hair tousled, sweaty, and left to her fate with a severe asthma attack. When Manssur was left alone in the house, he opened the door to the bedroom where his wife lay almost breathless, entered sadistically, and staring at her with a fixed gaze like that of a revolver and yellow feline eyes, he showed her the inhaler and asked her insolently and aggressively:

"Where is Hassna?"

52

She couldn't speak, she was motionless, as if paralyzed, only moving her head from side to side. He looked like an erupting volcano spewing lava from his mouth, and suddenly she stopped breathing. Manssur shook her violently, trying to revive her, but it was useless. He called the ambulance, and when they arrived, it was too late; Lalla had died. He told the nurse that his wife hadn't been able to find her inhaler, that she was always losing it. He told them that the maid had gone out shopping and that he had heard her in the distance, but when he arrived, it was too late.

He signed the death certificate. Manssur waited for Amal, the maid, to arrive so that she could begin the funeral rites, since the deceased was a woman and a woman had to perform the ritual.

When Amal came home after shopping, she saw the ambulance leaving, went into the house, and found out what had happened. As she entered the room, the sun cast a yellowish-amber light that flickered on the floor where Lalla lay, pale and lifeless like a porcelain doll. Amal was surprised that this tragedy had occurred after she had heard a fight in the bedroom, a loud slam of the door, and the master had sent her to do the shopping. But there was nothing to be done; her mistress was in the kingdom of Allah, and she would prepare her for the wake and burial.

On the way to Azrou.

Hassna had drunk a lot of liquid during the trip; her bladder was about to burst and she couldn't see anywhere along the road to stop and relieve herself. She reached the great cedar forest and pulled the van off the road. She saw that there was no one around and no cars passing by. She got out of the vehicle, took off her burqa, and was left in her Moroccan dress, a long tunic, and pants underneath. She found a leafy bush, crouched down, and emptied all the liquid inside her. She felt great relief in her bladder. When she came out of her hiding place, she approached the truck and was surprised to find that she was not alone. The truck was full of Barbary macaques that had entered through the window and were feasting on the cakes and sweets she had bought to eat during the trip. The monkeys were sitting on her burqa, eating happily and did not even flinch at Hassna's presence; they seemed to be used to seeing people and being fed.

Hassna was surprised and frightened. She grabbed a long branch to scare them away, but it was useless. The monkeys did not leave the vehicle. There was even a female monkey with her baby on her back. The presence of these noisy monkeys seemed to increase the midday heat, and a flame of impatience burned through her body. Hassna thought about waiting for them to finish eating and leave, but to her surprise, a truck approached and stopped next to hers. Hassna's blood ran cold when she saw that her hair and face were uncovered, and an intense wave of coldness invaded her body. Her face was covered with a mask of terror and she felt a cold chill in her stomach as she was drenched in adrenaline-induced sweat. The tension was so thick you could cut it with a chainsaw.

Suddenly, she saw that the occupants were two foreign girls. They got out of the truck and approached Hassna, greeting her in English. Hassna knew the language, and the girls introduced themselves: Rania Nazer, a 20-year-old Danish girl, and her friend Kristy, a 23-year-old Norwegian. They told her that they had come from Europe to visit Morocco for a month and were stopping at different places to get to know them. Finally, they wanted to reach Imlil, in the High Atlas, to climb the mountains, and then they would go camping in the Merzouga desert, with Marrakech as their final destination. At first, Hassna was nervous because they were looking for her and she was not wearing her burqa. She was afraid they would recognize her, but then she banished all negative thoughts when she learned that the girls had stopped because the area was famous for its Barbary macaques. The girls helped her get the monkeys out of the truck by lowering a basket of fruit and placing it on the ground. They opened the door, and when the monkeys saw the fruit, they quickly left, freeing up the truck. After eating, the monkeys were unfazed by the human presence and lay motionless, face up on the grass, sunbathing.

Hassna thanked them effusively and they stayed with the monkeys, taking photos while Hassna shook her burka and the seats, which were covered in crumbs.

Hassna told them that she was also getting to know Morocco, that her mother's family was from those lands, without mentioning the real reason that had brought her there.

For the moment, Hassna thought it reasonable to get to know these girls. In the absence of Omar and Rania, she felt accompanied. Her sadness was inside her. They were always on her mind, and nostalgia overwhelmed her when she remembered the day of her failed wedding and the twist of fate, and she thought for a moment to calm her anguish.

Inga, the Danish girl, invited Hassna to take a walk around Imlil to climb mountains 1,800 meters above sea level. Below, on the mountainside, there were beautiful valleys, small villages, livestock, streams, and walnut trees.

Kristy told Hassna that Mount Toubkal was the highest, at 4,167 meters above sea level. They couldn't climb it in winter because it would be covered in snow.

Hassna thought about it and agreed to accompany them.

"But I don't have any climbing gear," Hassna added.

"Don't worry, we have plenty of climbing gear," insisted Kristy, who seemed very excited about her new friend, who spoke English, Spanish, Arabic, Berber, and several dialects.

Hassna wanted to send a message to Rania about the adventure she was about to embark on, but there was no signal.

The three girls set off for Imlil in two vehicles, one behind the other. Hassna felt safer traveling with someone. They set off past humble whitewashed adobe houses, where a bonfire burned under a small forest of villages and smoky, sordid chimneys appeared from small, humble houses with decrepit ochre facades bathed in a dusty light.

Along the way, some men wore white robes and a small cap called a kufi, a typical African headdress, while others wore yellow turbans wrapped around their heads. They passed through rugged, rocky mountains, rugged landscapes, and dry desert plains full of rocks and gravel, as well as mosques, where they saw many shoes abandoned outside the entrance gate.

Before beginning the ascent, they decided to stop at a small shop to stock up on food and water. The foreign girls had brought a tent to camp and sleep on the slopes of the Atlas Mountains.

Hassna was very excited about her new friends. Above all, it distracted her and made her forget her cruel fate. Until now, she had managed to control the torrent of suffering; this was a small respite from the other stormy part that fate had in store for her.

Together they fixed up the trucks and packed their belongings, blankets, and supplies. It was very cold at night, and since they had no heating, they had to put on lots of warm clothes.

They set off for the mountains. The road was rocky. They passed adobe houses, orchards, and green valleys with beautiful crops. It was an ideal time to climb since it was autumn. Winter was not the best month, as the mountains would be covered with snow. They carried a first-aid kit with pills for altitude sickness and remedies for minor injuries.

They found a good spot and camped at the foot of a mountain. Hassna planned to sleep in her truck for more privacy, while the girls would sleep in their tent. They agreed to leave early as they had many hours of travel ahead of them. This was all an adventure for Hassna. At night, they made a campfire; the place was deserted under a large Mercury moon that embraced the mountain. They shared provisions and told Hassna details and stories of their mountaineering experiences. The girls drank wine, except for Hassna, whose religion did not allow it. Everything was in darkness, and the only light was that of the moon. They lent Hassna a flashlight so she could see at night in case she needed to leave the vehicle. The word "freedom" seemed to make sense to Hassna.

When the sun went down, the night fell so deep that they couldn't even see their hands. With flashlights, everyone went to their tents and vehicles to sleep, curling up under thick blankets.

Early in the morning, the girls made coffee and invited her to breakfast. She brought cheese, honey, and bread to share. After breakfast, each gathered her equipment and they set off on a short hike. Hassna wore her hair tied back in a ponytail; since they were all women and there were no men in sight, she didn't need to wear a veil. She felt free, breathing in the fresh air. They climbed the rocky mountain; the small stones were as sharp as blades. She walked carefully, doing very well despite it being her first time. Hassna stopped next to a hamada in an unknown place among thorny plants and wild trees, found a clear spot, sat down, and asked the girls to continue without her, as she was very tired and would wait for them there when they came down.

Hassna rested, enjoying the beautiful view from above, breathing in the fresh air and delighting in the sight of the valleys, palm trees, little houses, and red mountains of the High Atlas. The austere moors and cheerful streams offered a wonderful view.

The girls appeared a few hours later, coming down from the mountain, fascinated by the beautiful experience.

"Are you feeling better, Rania?" Kristy asked.

"Better now," replied Hassna, "I enjoyed these beautiful views and even had time for a nap. I got tired very quickly and I doubt I can climb Mount Toubkal. The truth is that tomorrow I will begin my journey back. I am very sorry I cannot accompany you. After breakfast we will say goodbye, it has been a pleasure to meet you."

Kristy was saddened by Hassna's decision, but she understood her concern; she didn't have the physical strength to climb mountains, let alone Toubkal.

Once down, they showed Hassna the photos they had taken on the mountain. She smiled happily at each photo, showing her perfect white teeth.

"How beautiful, it's a shame I missed it, but I felt too ill to continue. I didn't want to be a hindrance to you, so I preferred to rest."

They joyfully enjoyed the beautiful spectacle of the sunset over the immensity of the Sahara, illuminated by a twilight of warm reddish, green, and orange tones, where caravans of Bedouins riding dromedaries could be seen in the distance, in a landscape of desolation, stillness, and peace; a grandiose desert setting.

Happy, they retired to wash and prepare the fire for dinner. It was getting dark and they wanted to go to bed early. Hassna had planned to leave early in the morning for the Merzouga desert, to sleep in the famous tents in the middle of the desert and enjoy a night of stars and a full moon. The girls would continue on to Toubkal, where they would meet up with the group arriving from Marrakech for the excursion to Mount Toubkal.

Hassna, after having dinner with the girls—tuna, bread, cheese, and dates—went to sleep in her 4x4, very tired and hoarse from talking so much.

The next morning, she woke up with sore legs from the effort of climbing the mountain. She got out of the truck and headed to her friends' tent for breakfast and to say goodbye. The tent was closed, so she called out to them.

"Inga, Kristy, wake up. Let's have breakfast."

No one answered. She thought they might have gone for a walk around the area, or that they were still sleeping. She approached the tent and saw that the zipper was slightly open on one side. She peered through a gap and froze, a terrifying chill shaking her to her core. Her heart was pounding and her body was shaking with nerves, her pupils dilated like saucers. She felt as if an axe had been driven into her sternum. She had not expected such a sight and was stunned by the nightmarish scene.

The girls' throats had been slit, their bloody bones were visible, and there was blood spattered everywhere. She didn't want to see any more. She remained in a state of shock, petrified, and at the same time thinking about running away as quickly as possible. Her body trembling, she let out a bloodcurdling scream that echoed through the mountains. A feeling of revulsion and horror invaded her body. Horrified by the gruesome sight, her legs began to weaken and she felt her bones crumble like sand. She turned around and impulsively, vomited and fell to the ground. No matter how hard she tried to calm down, she couldn't control her nerves. Her heart was beating so fast that it felt like it was going to jump out of her chest. She was aware of the gravity of the situation. She didn't think twice, as there was nothing she could do for them, and she staggered back to the vehicle, trying to get out of there as quickly as possible. Her friends had had their throats slit while they were resting in the tent. The scene was gruesome: the tent splattered with blood and the two girls with their throats cut from side to side. The blood glistened like brushstrokes of red paint everywhere.

She ran frantically to the 4x4, determined as if a cobra were stalking her. She felt tightness in her chest and throat. She swallowed, her throat dry as she tried to control the panic that was overwhelming her. She looked around; there was no one in sight, only the roar of the wind.

Hassna wondered who could have done such a barbaric thing. Why them?

The night before, Hassna had curled up in the back of the truck, covered with black blankets up to her head to keep warm. Maybe that's why they didn't see her and thought they were alone in the tent. She wondered when it had happened.

"I didn't hear any noise. I was exhausted from the walk and fell asleep as soon as I lay down."

She started the truck's engine and drove away as if the fury of the accelerator were her vengeful hand leaving the scene of the crime. There was nothing she could do; she couldn't even serve as a witness since she hadn't seen or felt anything. They were completely dead, and she had to keep running. Staying would only make her situation worse.

She left the place with the veil covering her face, heading towards the desert, trying to control her body. She didn't know how much time had passed since the tragedy. She drank water from her canteen, trembling, with something horrible boiling in her chest like the roar of an explosion that shatters everything into a thousand pieces. She felt that all those excesses were stalking her, that danger was relentlessly following her. She thought it best not stop to make friends and stayed away from their path. In the midst of it all despite the anguish that gripped her she felt free and fortunate to be alive. Breathing fresh air renewed her from within even with the deep sorrow she felt for her murdered Friends. She looked at her map; it would take her approximately seven and a half hours to reach her destination, since she strayed out of the way by follow the girls up the mountain.

She began to see dunes, which looked like a huge golden sea. From time to time she saw dromedaries eating tamaris, a bush that grows in the desert and grazing on grass, and even cacti with their large spines. Hassna could appreciate the beauty of the motionless dunes, the fine quiet sand and the clear blue cloudless sky. The peace and quiet of the desert calmed her, despite her pain. However, her soul was agitated, not knowing if she would make it back to the tents before nightfall.

She continued her journey using her map and tried to travel in a straight line. Along the way, there were small tents belonging to nomads who lived in the desert with their small herds of goats. They traveled, settling anywhere until they found a watering hole. On weekends, they took their animals to the souk to sell them. The Drawa Berbers lived in the Draa River valley. The dadès of the northeast, in the High Atlas, crossed the desert on dromedaries. Hassna tried to distract her mind by contemplating the landscape, always alert in case someone was following her, controlling the fear that accompanied her.

Granada

After Lalla's burial, Manssur ordered Amal to remove all of his wife's belongings from the bedroom and donate them.

"I want that room empty and clean," Manssur insisted, radiating a stench of rage that hung in the air. Then he disappeared into the shadows with the speed of a cat. He was a man as cold as a rattlesnake in heat.

"Yes, sir," Amal replied, feeling very confused. Manssur withdrew his sinister figure with firm, hurried steps that made the floor creak.

Amal, who always tidied up her mistress's things, began sadly packing her robes, scarves, blouses, and shoes into boxes. When she was finishing, she saw a note inside a slipper. It was addressed to her. The paper was folded and read: "Amal, give this to Rania discreetly." Amal shuddered as she read the note, took it, and hid it in her pocket. When she finished her task and Manssur left, she called Rania and told her that her mistress had left her a letter. Since Rania knew that a detective was spying on her, she couldn't go pick it up, and Amal couldn't deliver it to her. Rania gave her address and asked Amal to put it in an envelope and mail it.

Taking advantage of Manssur's absence, Amal went to the post office and sent it by express mail. She returned home and began doing her household chores. Manssur arrived and checked Lalla's room, which was empty and clean, and her belongings were in boxes to be donated, except for her jewelry, which Manssur had kept in the safe.

He was very upset and in a bad mood because his niece had not shown up, and neither the police nor the detective had any news or results, even though the detective spent his time spying on Rania's house, following her everywhere and stalking her house like a restless animal waiting for its prey.

Desert

Hassna drove fast, calculating that she would arrive at 5:30 p.m. The 4x4 sped across the desert until it ran out of fuel. She had an hour and forty-five minutes to go when the truck stopped in the desert.

Panicked at the sight of her murdered friends, she forgot that she should have refilled the gas tank and brought the spare fuel can, and set off without thinking twice. No one was passing by on the dune road, so she grabbed her water can, got out of the vehicle and began walking for as long as she had left.

She set off, trying to cross the golden dunes with feet as light as mercury, quickly and without stopping but her legs sore from the previous day, sank up to her calves in the soft sand, making it very difficult for her to move forward. Indifferent to her fatigue, she did not stop to rest; she summoned insolent strength to walk on the sand, dismembering her bare feet as they moved silently. It was hellishly hot but she did not slow down despite being lost and fearful that the windy night would come and the clouds of sand would block her path. She kept going, crawling like an insect under the solemn grandeur of the desert. Suddenly, a warm wind rose brushing against some stunted palm trees. The memory of recent events had settled in her mind, and the terrifying images from inside her friends' tent were present. She feared that the killers would find her, since she had abandoned the truck on the mountainside that night, and that when they saw her, they would recognize her catch her walking defenselessly, and kill her like her friends.

The sound of the wind rustled the palm trees. No matter how hard she tried, she made very little progress. Her legs hurt, and the effort of walking made them feel even worse. She walked against the heat of the sunset, through the hardened glass of her misfortune, on the soft sand, with the afternoon sun at her back. She felt restless from the turmoil she had endured in recent months; her memories mingled confusedly in the immensity of the Sahara.

Suddenly, she saw the light of the setting sun barely announcing itself, and the sky turned a deep red. That fiery, overwhelming red settled on the horizon, exploding with changing colors like a soft lament of loose sand. The purple and violet clouds were lost on the horizon in the blue of the sky, the beauty of the landscape contrasting with her suffering. She looked at the glow of the sky that had begun to fade; on another occasion, it would have been a delight to her eyes, but at that moment, she thought it was getting dark. She did not want to remain in the shadows.

Looking back she saw the truck. According to her, she had been walking for over an hour and felt she had made little progress, as the soft sand buried her tired legs up to her knees and each step was agony. That fateful afternoon, when not even the wind disturbed the silence of the sunset. The sun faded, cooling the hot afternoon, while clouds bubbled in the blue sky, the gentle wind lifted the sand in a gentle slope, and the few rays of sunlight played among the wide undulations of the dunes. The heat ceased with the sunset. The fleeting splendor of another minor day was gone forever, bristling the palm trees that gradually blended into the blackness of the desert.

The light was becoming diffuse, very faint and the shadows of the clouds were buried under the darkness of the night. His impassive, dull eyes pierced the dense darkness of the night. He shook off his catastrophic thoughts, stumbling over his own stale breath, and felt fear curling around him like a vine, while the moon shone like a silver nail among the millions of stars above his head. There was more silence, as if a moan emerged from the soul of those dunes.

She continued walking under a Mediterranean night with a starry sky and darkness interrupted by moonlight, which illuminated the golden, undulating dunes of fine sand.

The stars of the night offered her a darkness carpeted with a hemorrhage of diamonds in the sky, sprouting in the night.

Suddenly, the full moon had conquered the darkness of the night. All she could do was keep going, accompanied only by the moonlight, humbly bowing to the desert, hoping it would allow her to escape alive to somewhere or find some nomadic dwelling that would take her in. Her white robe stood out in the darkness. She walked and walked, overcome with fear as the impending darkness surprised her. She could see and hear nothing beyond the dunes of fine golden sand, where her shoes had sunk from the beginning, and she could not find them. She felt helpless, certain that the night would be eternal. Frightened and fearful she walked aimlessly, feeling completely defenseless with her veil whipped by the wind and sand. She felt lost in the desert. With her huge, bright eyes covered in tears, she moved forward in a sad state of oppression and sadness, and every time her eyes took on a strange glow, her face was enveloped in the hijab that served as her protection as she walked.

The night was beautiful, and the moon shone softly. She began to walk with the steps of a large animal, but little by little she disappeared into the darkness. Then she felt as if her spirit were moth-eaten. She had no point of reference. She tried to perceive signs that would show her the way, but everything was the same.

The moon moved gently along a path of diamonds, illuminating the uncertain route. She walked panting with a deathly pallor, returning to the terrible hours of agonizing progress over the soft desert sand, walking in the unfortunate night, almost dying.

The moon's halo filled half the sky, the air was calm and the stars were in their places. Suddenly, the moon's glow had disappeared; someone had turned off the moon on the horizon. Everything became soft, silent, and dark.

"Omar, where are you?" she cried desperately, the words breaking like waves behind her.

Tears fell, clouding her vision. She wiped her eyes which were full of sand and tears, with her veil. Then she felt real pain total helplessness, the world collapsing around her   without warning or control. She plunged into the dark shadows with eyes glowing like starlight, trying to guide her way before returning to seek the moonlight. Meanwhile, the prevailing silence broke the loud beating of her heart.

Suddenly, a sandstorm broke out the wind whipping up the sand in a blinding whirlwind, lashing it against her robe and the scarf she had used to protect her eyes. She felt a deep sense of oppression; her throat was irritated by the sand, her lips cracked from dryness, and even her tongue was swollen. The wind whistled and the moment of silence disappeared. She sat motionless, hiding her head between her legs, holding it with her arms, and wrapped herself in sadness curling up like a wounded animal.

At night, the temperature dropped dramatically. She had no shelter other than the tunic she was wearing. She had no shoes, no strength her legs hurt, she was hungry, and her future was uncertain. Her eyes felt irritated.

Hassna, in her helplessness, cried out: "I want to disappear into the fine golden sand of the desert, bury my soul and lose myself in infinity, my body collapses to await the end."

He remained motionless until the endless night passed.

The sands surrounding the desert absorbed the echo of his voice, which sank into the deep sands of the desert.

Granada

Rania received the letter Amal had sent her. Intrigued by the unexpected missive, she opened it and sat down to read it. She read the letter with great anticipation, her heart beating fast; she was eager to share it with the court. She found endless unpleasant revelations, which could have been foreseen if Lalla had shared the ordeal of her life. In the letter, Lalla recounted what had happened:

Rania, if anything happens to me, I need you to seek justice. Manssur has locked me in my room and taken away my inhaler so that I cannot breathe when I have an asthma attack. He is torturing me because he wants me to tell him where Hassna is. I will not tell him anything, so I know that my end is near. I am writing this letter

66

so that you know that if anything happens to me, if I die of an asthma attack, it is Manssur's fault.

Take care of Hassna and thank you for your help.

Lalla Sabal.

Rania was stunned. He had killed her. She thought that if this were Morocco, he would be sentenced to death, but in Spain it would be life imprisonment for kidnapping and murder. "I have to talk to dad," she thought. She put the letter away and called her father, who was a lawyer.

Rania arrived at her father's office, located at 7 Trajano Street. She entered a luxurious building that housed the Nazer law firm. Rania's father belonged to the most prestigious and wealthy Moroccan family; they exported refined petroleum products, as well as Marak and Nazer Motors cars.

The secretary came out to greet her and accompanied her to her father's office. They hadn't seen each other for several months; her father traveled a lot and they only spoke on the phone. He was very happy to see her looking so beautiful. They hugged, and Rania told him about her friend Hassna's situation: her confinement in the psychiatric hospital, the abuse by the doctor, who subjected her to electric shocks and strong jets of water, and kept her drugged and tied down in a straitjacket in case she disobeyed. She told him how she had rescued her with the help of aunt Lalla and finally showed him the letter in which she held Manssur responsible if anything happened to her. It later emerged that Manssur was in cahoots with the center's doctor to keep Hassna hospitalized indefinitely so that he could keep the inheritance.

Rania's father listened to his daughter's story, read the letter and asked her if she could find more evidence and witnesses. She had Amal as a witness who had heard a fight before Manssur sent her to do the shopping and when she returned, Lalla was dead. The other witness was Rania, who saw the state her friend was in, being treated like a madwoman. Hassna could easily pass the psychological test of being completely sane and capable of managing her inheritance.

Rania's father, knowing that Hassna's uncle was a compulsive gambler, suspected that he might have embezzled his niece's inheritance for his own benefit. Rania asked her father to keep the letter in a safe place, as Manssur had a private detective following her, spying on her every move because he thought she had Hassna hidden somewhere.

Rania's father promised her that he would take care of the case and that he would be happy to help her friend put an end to her ordeal.

Rania said goodbye to her father with a hug and a kiss, thanking him for the favor.

Desert

Hassna woke up curled up next to a tamarisk bush. She had taken refuge there during the night to protect herself from the sandstorm. She didn't think about the possibility of being stung by a scorpion, a snake, or a fox. She was so tired that she surrendered to her fate.

The sky began to clear and the stars faded away. It was dawn; the dark night was behind her, the new day was dawning over the desert before sunrise, the morning twilight was appearing; it was dawn or sunrise.

Little by little, the red color of the sky turned to gold and the edge of the sun slowly appeared. Despite everything, she felt optimistic about the future and walked with inconceivable energy, drawing strength from where she had none. She hadn't eaten in twelve hours. Suddenly, she realized she was lost in the vastness of the Sahara. The map was leading her nowhere; everything looked the same. She had walked a long way; according to her she should have arrived somewhere by now. She continued walking in a straight line. The morning dragged on with hot, lazy hours; she didn't know where she was going. She felt a pang of anguish that caused a sudden attack of anxiety. The sadness of the previous day turned into exhaustion and despair.

Suddenly it was noon, and the sun was shining brightly in the clear blue sky. It was right above her, the fierce midday sun strong and unbearable. Hassna had almost no water left; she could see and hear nothing beyond the sand dunes, and the sun was scorching. She couldn't stand the heat on her face, so she pulled the veil covering her head over her face, leaving only her eyes exposed, thus protecting herself from the sun and sand. But the scorching heat suffocated her. Her feet burned. From time to time, she would stop among the bushes to mitigate the heat from the burning sand on her feet, which burned like live fire. The wear and tear of the hours in the sun was impossible to bear, and the tunic protected her from the sun, but it suffocated her with the heat and prevented her from walking.

She tried to keep going, feeling a heat that puffed like a cauldron, her heart beating as slowly as when she slept, and something terrible pressing on her chest. Her face, reddened by fever, looked pale; she had lost much of her beauty.

She threw her spirit into the wind so that it would disappear into the desert horizon, be renewed, and return clean and pure, trying to continue living. She saw a small tent in the distance; it was like an oasis shining in the darkness of her soul. The summer sun scorched her, and she continued walking on the burning sand.

Could it be a mirage?

Her body trembled, and she felt as if she were floating in a void, not knowing if it was from the cold or from fear. She cried so much that, unable to hold back the tears of regret any longer, she continued walking through the warm sand dunes until she found the oasis of lost love.

"I feel like I'm fading away, weak, faltering soon my soul (Nafs) will float out of my body into the air, so that later my body will succumb among the sands of the desert," she thought.

She kept walking, almost without strength, wandering aimlessly until she reached nowhere. The loneliness of this arid and scorching world kept her going until her body became lifeless. "I have no water, only the few tears that evaporate as I walk. My heart is devoid of love. I am sad and dejected: first my parents, my home, then Omar and Rania. I need to abandon myself to this loneliness among the dunes and the wind. My tears dry up, my tired feet burn, I will surrender to the sands of the desert and it will be the end of a lost dream, my body loses the strength to wait..."

Hassna's body collapsed like leaves from a tree in autumn.

In the distance, a Moroccan boy riding a dromedary was approaching. He wore a blue tunic (suriyah) with elaborate yellow embroidery on the collar and cuffs. He wore a yellow turban wrapped around his head. He approached a white lump he saw in the sand. When he was close enough, he dismounted to inspect what was in the sand. He approached curiously, trying to help the wandering person. Then he saw a woman lying down. He removed her enchanted veil as if touching a flower with sacramental gentleness. She was very young, a fragile creature with her rolled-up veil covering her face, her long black hair looking disheveled and full of sand. Barefoot and feverish, she could barely move. He looked at her with an open heart, with devotion and tenderness. When he took her pulse, he saw that she was very weak. Even so, she was alive, her breathing sandy and like the pale sweat of a dying woman. Carefully, he removed the veil that enveloped her, shook off the sand, and gave her water, then lifted her onto the dromedary and took her to the first nomad tent he found.

He lifted her down with his strong arms and carried her to the modest tent, patched and held up by sticks in the sand, the same one she had seen before she fainted. A nomadic Berber woman came out to meet them, greeted them carefully, and laid Hassna down on some worn and faded rugs on the floor of the small tent, which also served as a bedroom and was beginning to light up through a crack worn by the sapphire light of day.

She asked the woman if she had anything to bring the girl's fever down. The woman went to the well and brought back a bucket of fresh water. She placed damp cloths on Hassna's forehead, arms, and neck. She gave some of them fresh water to drink, wet her hair, changed the compresses as they warmed up, and tried to bring her fever down little by little.

She put water on to boil to make borji mint tea and brought a small glass to serve it from a teapot, pouring it from a height, and placed a small plate of honey and sesame cookies on a small table, which she offered to the traveler.

Hassna, with a lost look in her eyes, seemed very tired, dirty, exhausted, fragile, and in pain; her muscles were shattered, and her brain burned with fever like fire. Her pulse was racing, her skin was red, she was dizzy, dry-mouthed, and had a severe headache. Her face looked frightened and helpless; she couldn't coordinate her thoughts and was babbling, her hand looking like a corpse abandoned to its fate. When she opened her large, dark, almond-shaped eyes, her gaze was erratic, her lips dry and cracked, about to bleed. Hamid moistened them as he asked her:

"What's your name? Where are you going? Where are you from? Are you sleepy? Don't close your eyes, don't fall asleep."

He wouldn't let her sleep, turning her face away to clear her mind and moistening her eyebrows. Hours passed and Hamid cared for her, watching her, reading the grief in her spirit until she opened her tired eyes . She woke up surrounded by shadows and unfamiliar faces. She tried to move her limbs, battered by exhaustion, without knowing where she was. He smiled at her with his white teeth. Disoriented, she looked at him with her warm gaze and dreamy eyelashes that made the sand breathe. In a second, she enveloped him with the incomparable sparkle of her almond-shaped eyes and made him feel warmth in his soul. She looked at him silently, with an inexplicable expression on her face, shaken by uncertainty.

The woman had taken Hamid into her modest home and cared for him. He was grateful for the gesture of the woman who, together with her husband, made a living from selling their flock of sheep, which she took to the village to sell in the souk of the medina and bring food to her family. The small shop offered not only love, but also the invisible murmur of sadness, poverty and helplessness, but they gladly offered what little they had to help the pilgrim, as was the law of the desert.

Hamid asked the couple if they could keep her that night; she was too delicate to take her to the health center, as it was very late and it would soon be dark. They agreed, and Hamid promised to return early the next day to pick her up. He said goodbye to them and furtively caressed Hassna's cheek with the back of his hand.

Hamid was of Berber origin, tall, handsome, with masculine features, a strong build, broad shoulders, an elongated face, a straight nose, dark skin, slightly wavy black hair, a thick black beard, large dark eyes as bright as olives, a noble smile, and teeth as white as snow. He had a strong, deep, and enigmatic gaze. He was about twenty-five years old. His family were farmers and his father owned the Luxury Tents Hotel. Across a vast expanse of desert, there were several dozen of these hotels. Inside, there was a large dining room and a living room for guests, mostly foreigners or wealthy people who traveled to explore the Sahara, ride dromedaries, and listen to desert music. The tents were luxurious inside; the rooms had sand floors covered from end to end with brightly colored African rugs. There was a large bed with two nightstands with lamps on either side. On one side was the private bathroom, fully equipped with hot water and all the amenities. The room had natural light and was tastefully decorated. The jaimas were large tents where visitors stayed. There were tents for one person, for couples, or for more people. They were arranged in a large circle, and at the back there was a large tent that served as a dining room with several individual tables for two, four, six, or more people, arranged around two large tables in the center. The buffet served a variety of Afro-Moroccan dishes. Guests came to serve themselves and then returned to their tables to enjoy the exotic food. Everywhere you looked, there was a profusion of luxury items.

They were served by very dark-skinned Africans, luxuriously dressed in their traditional costumes. The dining tent featured exotic African décor, covered from end to end with beautiful rugs with geometric designs and bright colors.

On the large buffet table were chicken tagines, vegetable tagines, and meat tagines, each in its own clay pot with its original pointed lid. Couscous was also served, accompanied by lamb or beef and vegetables, served with wheat semolina and presented on a platter to be shared at the table in the traditional style. There was also Arabic rice with chicken and almonds, or the mixed dish with Arabic rice, kibbeh, tabbouleh, and grape and cabbage rolls.

These dishes were accompanied by plums, dates, raisins, sesame seeds, sweet and sour almonds, honey, and cinnamon. On the dessert table, displayed its basic ingredients: honey, almonds, pistachios, and sesame seeds flavored with orange or rose water.

Hamid, the second of two brothers, had been sent to Spain by his father to study. He was a lawyer and spent a few days visiting the area. That day, he was out for a walk to see the jet-black Arabian horses and golden bay horses his father bred when he found Hassna collapsed on the road.

Granada

Rania's father called her to inform her that her friend Hassna's case was going well. With the letter Lalla had left and the two witnesses, it would be enough to win the case and send Manssur to prison for life, as well as the doctor who agreed to declare Hassna insane.

Rania did not know how to contact her. She would first have to get her passport to meet up with her, as there was no cell phone coverage where her friend was.

Desert

Early in the morning, Hassna woke up disoriented inside a nomad tent wearing different clothes, faded clothes that were not hers. She looked around and saw no one. After a while, the woman who had helped her appeared, bringing mint tea in a small jug and a small glass.

Hassna thanked her, got up with difficulty, and asked her how she had gotten there. She couldn't remember anything; she felt as if she were in an unknown dimension and her heart was heavy.

The woman explained that a young man from the desert had found her, brought her there, and kept her company for most of the day, waiting for her to recover. He had left at dusk and would return early in the morning to pick her up.

The woman had changed her sweaty clothes that night. She arrived early, bringing her washed and dried clothes. Hassna put them on, combed her hair, and put on her veil or hijab. She thanked her for her hospitality and had tea with cakes and dates. Hassna's feet were covered with wet rags, which the woman changed carefully so as not to burst the blisters and to care for the skin torn from walking so much on the hot sand. The small room was filled with the smell of burning wood.

Hamid arrived early, riding his dromedary. He approached her as if in a dream. He found Hassna much better. She looked at Hamid with a heart broken by pain, looking at him with her sad, luminous eyes. He sensed that she was haunted by a fateful dream. Her silent savior had arrived, appearing in her life like water in the desert. She did not know his name or what he was doing there. Hassna, with newfound curiosity, asked him.

"Where did you find me? What happened to me? Where am I? How much time has passed?"

Hamid took her in his arms, his face gallant and tender. He felt her delicate, well-manicured hands and told her how he had found her and taken her to the nearest shop.

"You've been delirious since yesterday at noon. I thought you were going to die. What happened to you? Did you get lost?"

Hassna told him that the 4x4 truck had run out of fuel and that, since he still had an hour and forty-five minutes to go, he thought he could make it on foot.

"Where were you going?"

"My final destination was the tent city."

Hamid smiled and didn't tell her that she was his family. He gazed at her clean, fresh, youthful face, a beautiful capuli-colored face with original features and a virginal appearance, her long, silky black hair covered by the hijab that he had already discovered in the delirium of the previous day when they rescued her. Upon meeting her, a feeling awakened in him, as he saw her more beautiful than the sun.

"Do you feel strong enough to make it to the tents?"

"I feel fine, thanks to you and these kind people," replied Hassna, initiating a silent dialogue, finally feeling a dawn rising within her.

Hamid stared at her intently, his gaze deep, scrutinizing the abyss of her beautiful, large eyes that shone with intense warmth, and suddenly he felt the deep ardor of her gaze. That casual glance would lead to a turbulent but uncertain future love.

"I am doing my duty to help," replied the boy. "In the desert, we are altruistic."

Hassna observed his feelings.

"I wish all men were like you," Hassna replied, "there are many men unlike you, and because of one of them, I am here."

Hassna felt uneasy about that penetrating, fixed gaze of black eyes that barely blinked; she felt as if he were watching her.

Hamid noticed Hassna; her sensual lips and beautiful large eyes unsettled him.

She whispered to him with a welcoming smile, responding in a warm voice.

"I want to leave, but my feet hurt when I walk, and I left my things in the 4x4 truck that's stuck in the middle of the desert without fuel."

"Don't worry, I'll take care of your vehicle and send you your suitcase and clothes. For now, we can only thank these people for their hospitality."

"Shukran. Thank you, see you soon," Hamid and Hassna said to the couple who had taken them in. Hamid thanked them by giving them a few dirhams.

Hamid helped Hassna climb onto the dromedary. The contact with her warm body caused a wave of desire to wash over him.

"What is happening to me with this girl? I am attracted to her and I don't even know anything about her. She has beautiful eyes and a clear, transparent gaze," thought Hamid.

He felt the blood rushing through his veins. He stared at the golden dunes without saying a word, silently absorbing the attraction.

The sun rose again, setting and suffocating in a circle of red and orange; it was the birth of a splendid day, in which the dunes stood out against the golden background of the sands, illuminating the silent desert.

Occasionally, a nomad's tent could be seen with smoke rising from a fire, announcing lunchtime. She realized that her clothes had taken on that same smoky aroma.

It was a thirty-minute walk from where she was to the tents. Hassna remained spellbound, appreciating the shimmering, flutter r of the intense blue of an oceanic sky with white clouds and the beauty of the desert. It was something she had wanted to flee and forget just days ago, along with the macabre memory of the foreign girls, carrying with her the lost breath of all hope.

Although she did not know Hamid, she felt protected by him for showing solidarity and concern for saving her life. Her soul was filled with gratitude to him and to Allah for giving her life back.

Riding a dromedary over the intense ochre of the desert, the white tents, the landscape, the horizon of dunes, and the clear blue sky merged into a single line that made her shiver.

Hamid was a native of the area; he knew everything about the desert, including the climate, the terrain, and the nomadic customs. They finally reached their destination and helped Hassna down from the dromedary. He was surprised again when he touched her skin. She needed to rest, rehydrate, and treat the blisters on her feet. She still felt tired and weak, but at last she could breathe the fresh air of freedom.

The manager came out to greet her and informed her that they had been waiting for her for two days, as she had made the reservation in advance. Hassna told him that she had had an accident during the trip.

Hamid and a young man known as "Rasta Boy" because of his multiple braids typical of Rastafarians accompanied her to her tent. He informed Hassna that her small luggage would arrive soon. After showing her the tent, he helped her to the dining room for the traditional welcome mint tea, accompanied by sweets typical of the Afro-Muslim area, also influenced by Mediterranean, Eastern, and African traditions. There were basic ingredients such as honey, almonds, pistachios, walnuts, coconut, and sesame, flavored with rose or orange blossom water.

After resting and enjoying mint tea (borgi) with almond cakes and dates, Hamid came to the dining room to tell her that her 4x4 truck with her belongings would arrive soon. Hassna had no words to express her gratitude for such kindness. Hamid smiled at her and told her that the people of the desert were helpful and very hospitable.

Hamid carefully took her to his luxurious tent, helping her to stay on her feet as she walked with difficulty due to the blisters on her feet. Then he said goodbye with the promise to see her again soon and left her to rest.

Hamid spoke privately with Rasta Boy and ordered him to take care of her and that she would be his responsibility.

The reddish-orange light of the sun began to herald the arrival of twilight. The last rays of sunlight languished over the purple mantle of dusk, and the sky was as scarlet as spilled paint.

Hassna was in her tent, lying on her bed, resting and letting the waters of anguish flow so that, in time, the river would carry her suffering to the sea.

Two hours later, Rasta Boy brought her small luggage.

"Shukran, for caring for me, good boy," Hassna said as she gathered her belongings.

"I inform you, miss, that the dining room is ready for dinner."

Hassna replied that she was not going to have dinner, that her feet hurt a lot and she preferred not to walk. The boy remembered that Hamid had told him to take good care of the girl. Half an hour later, he came back with a tray of food: falafel, chickpea and lentil croquettes covered with sesame seeds and drizzled with r labneh sauce. He also left her some ointment to soothe the burns on her feet.

"Miss, I brought you these snacks in case you get hungry later. I'm also leaving you some mint tea. If you don't want it, I'll pick it up later."

"Shukran, Rasta Boy," Hassna replied.

Hassna couldn't shake her memories, especially at night. She had risked a lot to get there, and it hadn't been easy. Her nerves were on edge. She had trouble falling asleep, and when she did, she would wake up sweaty, screaming and crying, wrapped in nightmares. She had been brutally beaten by the scorching sun, sweating with fear, feeling the hustle and bustle of silent travelers in the darkness. She didn't like the arrival of a new day and living her harsh reality. She wasn't safe yet.

"How long will this horror invade my soul day and night?" she wondered, thinking of her murdered friends.

Due to recent events, she was reluctant to make friends with strangers. During her stay in the desert, she was simply friendly, but kept people at a distance by appearing shy and withdrawn towards the other guests, often staying in her tent and not going out to the dining room.

Rasta Boy was a nice young man who cared about his customer and came to see how she was doing, if she was okay or if she needed anything. He brought her food and chatted with her when appropriate.

It was getting dark, and Hassna heard Berber drums and singing. It reminded her of her mother singing those beautiful songs. She looked outside her tent and saw all the guests sitting on logs in a semicircle. There was a mysterious atmosphere that drew her in. There were musicians playing instruments and singing. One of them was Rasta Boy. She quietly approached and sat down on a log to listen to them.

It was a magnificent full moon night dotted with stars. The logs to sit on were placed on beautiful magnificent rugs of bright colors with African designs. The musicians wore blue tunics with yellow trim on the cuffs and pointed collars, and blue turbans wrapped around their heads. In addition to the moonlight, torches illuminated all four sides, creating a unique and lively atmosphere. The echo of the music embraced the desert dunes, as the drums filtered through the sky and slid notes across the sand like gold dust. It was a moment of happy memories for Hassna.

Suddenly, Hamid arrived and sat down next to her. Hassna felt the fire of his gaze burning her, and a strange heat devoured her skin as if it were acid. She felt restless and her eyes resisted the moonlight. She blushed. Hamid's virile appearance intimidated her, but she did not move from his side, pretending to be cold and not revealing her feelings.

"What a beautiful moonlit night, isn't it?" Hamid asked.

Hassna replied with a smile, revealing her sensual lips beneath those large almond-shaped eyes, black as coal, which sparkled like two diamonds.

"Do you like music?"

"It brings back many memories of when I was a child," she replied, "my mother used to sing them, I think she missed the desert, her family and her customs."

"Was your father Berber?" asked Hamid.

"Arab Berber, but he was raised in Spain since he was a baby. My mother traveled to Spain when she was seventeen and stayed there. She met my father, they got married, and they went to live in Malaga, where I was born."

Hamid, admiring Hassna's charming smile and the beauty of her veil over her attractive face, stared at her and she blushed, lowering her head. He lifted her chin with his finger and when she looked at him, he said:

"I was admiring your beautiful face, which is etched in my memory."

Hassna felt her face flush, and then a pleasant silence fell between them.

Hamid felt a breath of spring toward her, mixed with a suppressed passion. The music ceased after midnight, and the bustle of musicians and spectators dispersed. The sleepy whispers dissipated, and the two sat under the glow of a moonbeam. She felt the pulse of her free will in her blood. Minutes later, someone turned off the moonlight. Then they slowly retired to rest. Hassna was helped by Hamid, whose touch on her arms made her shiver. He left her in her tent, bidding farewell to the evening with a warm, grateful smile.

That night, Hassna thought a lot about Hamid, about how handsome and attractive he was. Mentally, she ran her hands over his skin, feeling as if a strong draft of air was coming in through the window. She lay down in her large, soft bed and fell into a deep sleep.

The next morning she woke up very early, covered her face with her hijab to protect herself from the wind and sand, and went out to watch the sunrise. She was the only one awake; she found no one else outsi . She limped in front of her tent, barely able to put weight on the soles of her feet and walking on her heels. She sat on the sand to watch the sunrise, smiling like a beautiful woman.

Everything was shrouded in deep silence; she could even hear her own breathing. She appreciated that great sea of golden sand and thought that thanks to Hamid she was alive, and she remembered Omar.

"Could it be that he sent him from the afterlife to take care of me?" she thought.

Hassna went to the dining room and found no one there. She was returning to her tent when she ran into the Rasta boy. He greeted her and asked if she needed anything. She replied that she had gone out to watch the sunrise.

"Miss, I'm going to the dining tent to prepare everything for breakfast. If you'd like, you can come with me and I'll help you right away. Lean on me."

Hassna agreed.

The two entered the large dining tent, Hassna sat down, and the Rasta boy went to put water on to boil for the borji and prepared orange juice.

Rasta Boy, very attentive, offered her a newspaper, The Herald of Morocco, to leaf through while she waited for her mint tea.

Hassna was surprised to read the headline on the front page of the newspaper:

"Two foreign girls were found with their throats slit while resting in a tent on the slopes of an isolated mountain ten kilometers from Imlil, a small village in the High Atlas surrounded by vegetation and roads. They were found dead with signs of violence from a sharp weapon. Inga, a 20-year-old Danish national, and Kristy, a 23-year-old Norwegian national, according to a statement from the Ministry of the Interior. Moroccan authorities have suspended climbs to Mount Toubkal, the highest peak in the Atlas Mountains (4,167 meters), until further notice."

The newspaper published photos of their friends on the front page. Hassna shuddered, began to tremble, and continued reading.

"The girls embarked together on a month-long trip to the Moroccan city, a tourist attraction for mountaineering. Police found photos of these beautiful blonde girls with long hair and charming smiles posing for photos the day before."

Hassna thought, "Thank goodness I didn't take any photos with them, because otherwise I would be in serious trouble with the law because of my identity."

"Police in Rabat believe there may be a terrorist motive in southern Morocco. The bodies were transferred from the Marrakech morgue to Casablanca airport, from where they were repatriated to Norway and Denmark. This incident has frightened many tourists who had come to the region for mountaineering and they have left the area without completing their trip. Three suspects were arrested in Marrakech after being found in a valley in the High Atlas Mountains. So far, fifteen suspects have been arrested for the murder and face the death penalty."

After reading the alarming news in the newspaper, Hassna's body began to relax. She thanked Allah for once again saving her from death.

When Rasta Boy arrived with mint tea, orange juice, bread, honey, cheese, and dates, Hassna was pale as a ghost, trembling and hiding her condition as she looked at the newspaper and the news. Rasta Boy realized that the news had frightened her and thought that, since she had been rescued when she got lost in the desert, she might think she was in danger of dying on the road.

"Are you feeling unwell, miss?"

"No, Rasta Boy, the news has frightened me."

"You're safe here, miss. You're shaking, but don't worry, those criminals will be caught and they'll pay with their lives. There's no need to be afraid."

She nodded and asked Rasta Boy to bring her breakfast to her tent, as she had lost her appetite for the moment. "Maybe you'll feel like something later, miss."

"Shukran, Rasta Boy."

Rasta Boy was worried and thought it would be very difficult to find out what had really happened to Hassna.

Hassna arrived at her tent feeling restless, unable to avoid the anxiety-induced cramps that caused her to panic. She did not leave her tent all day.

Within minutes, night fell, a mask of fear and pain appeared on her face, and she did not sleep that night; she spent the whole night awake.

The wind whipped the tent canvas like a howl in the night. She stood with her eyes open, remembering with milky clarity a sinister landscape where shadows filtered through the silence of the night, until exhaustion overwhelmed her. She sank into dark thoughts, overcome by nostalgia. She woke up with large black circles under her eyes, like a raccoon.

She thought of Rania; she had lost her cell phone in the sands of the Sahara. She had to find a way to contact her and find out how things were going in Granada.

The next morning, she left the tent early and headed for the dining room. She found no one outside. She went in and saw the day's newspapers on a small table. She picked one up and sat down to see if she could find any more news about the murder of the foreign women.

"Investigations by the national police, the central gendarmerie, and the central investigation office are continuing," he read, "adding that the suspect was from the city of Marrakech, about sixty kilometers from Imlil, and that other suspects were being identified and searched for. Local witnesses reported that surveillance cameras at a nearby shelter detected three people who allegedly got out near the crime scene."

When Hassna read about the three people, she thought it might be the three of them and became nervous.

Police say a group known as the Lone Wolves, sympathizers of the Islamic group, was involved in the massacre. Authorities have identified a 25-year-old street vendor, Ablessamad Ejjoud, as the mastermind of the terrorist group. The group carried out the murder, which was aimed at attacking security forces and foreign tourists, as they focused on the town of Imlil, which is popular with tourists. During the raids, police found explosives, unauthorized hunting rifles, knives, and bomb-making materials. A week earlier, they had threatened to carry out a terrorist attack in a video. They filmed the moment of the beheading. During the filming, they describe their victims as enemies of Allah and claim that they are avenging their brothers who died in Syria. A Swiss-Spanish man is involved in teaching one of the detainees how to use communication tools, including new technologies, and training them in the use of firearms. The suspect followed an extremist ideology.

Hassna finished reading the newspaper, turning pale and gasping. Hassna saw Rasta Boy arrive, panting.

"Salam aleikum, miss."

"Aleikum salam, Rasta Boy," Hassna replied. "Why are you so tired?"

"Miss... with the latest events, many tourists are leaving without completing their stay. They are afraid to go out sightseeing and get killed, and others are frustrated because the hiking area is closed by the police, so I've been collecting guests' luggage and suitcases and loading them into vans so they can return home. This mountainous region is our only source of livelihood and that of many families, miss. The nearby mountains provide a livelihood for innkeepers, guides, dromedary and mule owners, and merchants. All of this is shaping up to be an economic crisis for the country."

"I'm so sorry, Rasta boy," Hassna replied.

"Tourism, miss, is the key to the Moroccan economy, as it accounts for ten percent of the country's wealth and is the second most important source of employment after agriculture."

"What a problem!" replied Hassna. "I'm so sorry."

"Yes, miss, those of us who work here are worried about losing our jobs. You'll see that we work hard so we won't get fired, but if we run out of tourists, the boss will be forced to let us go. Would you like me to bring you breakfast? Or would you prefer to serve yourself from the table?"

"Don't worry, I'm fine, I'll go and help myself at the table. I'd like to ask you where I can buy a cell phone. I need to call Spain."

"Well, miss, we don't sell them here in the desert, but I have a friend who does, although he's seven kilometers from here, in Khamlia."

"How can I get there? Could you take me in your truck?" Hassna asked anxiously.

"If you give me permission, we'll go, but by dromedary. The trucks are busy transporting tourists back to Tangier and it's a very long way."

"Okay, Rasta guy, I'm willing to go by dromedary."

"Have breakfast, miss, and then I'll tell you."

Hassna had breakfast as instructed by Rasta Boy, then retired to her tent to prepare for the journey. An hour later, the boy appeared, ready to take her.

"I'm ready. Will it be a problem to take me? Does your boss allow it?"

"Yes, miss, shall we go?"

They set off for the dunes on two dromedaries. Rasta Boy carried provisions of water and honey cakes with dates for the journey. He had also prepared a small backpack for Hassna with enough snacks for the trip.

They enjoyed the journey; the morning dawned with a bright and welcoming sun, the horizon displaying a symphony of pearly sand dunes that rose harmoniously as they traversed the desert in a friendly manner, the silence spreading like water in the ocean of sand.

They passed through a palm grove and came across nomadic tents and herds of dromedaries grazing. Despite everything, Hassna felt well protected in the middle of nowhere. She could only appreciate the beauty of the desert as the sun's rays caressed her beautiful face. They stopped and drank fresh water from their canteen. Rasta Boy added, "We're almost there, miss, we'll be in Khamlia soon."

Hassna's idea of having a phone and being able to communicate with Rania filled her with excitement and at the same time, she felt calm knowing what was happening with the problem of her escape.

During the trip, the Rasta boy told her about the city of Merzouga, located 150 meters above sea level in North Africa. It is a small city fifty kilometers from Algeria.

They walked through Berber villages and encountered people riding dromedaries wearing white tunics and kufi, a small round African cap on their heads.

The midday light was intense, the heat relentless. In front of the palm trees, they spotted a tent and dismounted from their dromedary to rest in a Berber nomad tent. They entered the small, patched canvas tent, supported by four poles. They went inside and sat down on a worn, faded old multicolored rug. A woman appeared with the usual borji: mint tea served in small glass cups, accompanied by traditional sweets. They rested for a while and then set off on their journey, leaving a tip for their hospitality. They were so poor that the only thing to be found was dust.

They continued their journey, and Rasta Boy told Hassna that most Moroccans are Berber-Arabs, or a mixture of both. They used to be Christians and later converted to Islam.

"Moroccan Berbers have curly black hair and dark skin; we are Africans (Amazighs)," said Rasta Boy. "Our king is called Mohammed VI, a member of the Alawite dynasty. He lives in Rabat and is working hard to improve the roads, provide good hotels, hostels, and all the amenities for visitors. He is also investing heavily in increasing tourism projects. 2008 was a record year for tourism, with eleven million visitors."

"We finally arrived in the city of Khamlia, known as the city of people blacker than oil, so called because its inhabitants are descendants of slaves."

"How interesting," added Hassna.

"Let's unload and tie up the dromedary," ordered Rasta Boy. Hassna looked around and saw many adobe buildings, palm trees, houses, and restaurants. As they were hungry, Rasta Boy suggested a place where they could eat a typical regional dish.

[The restaurant owner, a tal, dark- skinned, strong man, fell in love with Hassna and asked Rasta boy to exchange the girl for 20 dromedaries. Hassna paniked and told him she was engaged to be married].

They entered a restaurant called Deskgram, left their shoes outside, and entered a large room completely carpeted with several brightly colored rugs with cross patterns, placed side by side. The place was powered by solar panels. The owner of the restaurant, was a tall, burly African man a descendant of slaves, with teeth as white as a child's.

He wore an embroidered blue tunic and a yellow turban on his head, which stood out against his dark skin.

They entered the restaurant and sat down to eat on large cushions covered with brightly colored fabrics placed on the carpets. The walls were decorated with pink, orange, and blue fabrics with embroidery and fringes. The ceiling was made of cane and wood, and the lamps were made of wicker. The restaurant was surrounded by small round and rectangular maroon tables.

First, they brought the usual welcome teapot with borji, peanut and almond cakes.

The owner of the restaurant approached the table attentively to take our order. Rasta Boy ordered a typical Berber pizza. It was as big as a family-size pizza filled with vegetables and chicken, but covered with dough like a giant empanada. It was cut into triangles like pizzas. It was huge for two people, and they couldn't finish it.

The place was very nicely decorated. In the center of the dining room was a large column covered with dark brown fabric with light blue trim, forming round white patterns with African motifs.

After eating, Rasta Boy asked about his friend Said and was told that he was playing music in a white store a block away.

They arrived at the designated place and sat on brightly colored cushions—red, blue, yellow, and intense green—and the Gnawa music concert began. There were several African musicians with skin so dark that you could see the ivory inside their mouths. They wore white tunics and turbans with a red band crossed over their chests. They played drums, a cajon, a guitar, and maracas with sublime black euphoria. Some people who knew how to dance to African rhythms came closer, swaying to the beat of the music.

After the concert, the audience left the tent and Hassna also left. Rasta Boy approached Said to ask if he could sell him a cell phone. He agreed and asked him to accompany him to buy it. Rasta Boy signaled to Hassna that he would be right back and to wait for him a moment. She nodded and waited for him outside the tent, on a corner of the sidewalk next to the dance floor.

No more than five minutes had passed when a closed van pulled up. Two men got out and, impetuously and without consideration, dragged Hassna into the vehicle, covering her head and face with a sack. She tried to defend herself with suicidal ferocity, but to no avail. Her frantic excitement overwhelmed her with panic; her thoughts became confused and she did not know what was happening. She thought of the girls in Imlil, screaming in supplication. The van drove along winding roads, moving further and further away from the place.

When Rasta Boy returned, Hassna was gone. He searched everywhere for her and couldn't find her. He asked a person working on a construction site in front of the shop where Hassna had been waiting. The man told him that a van with two unknown men and another man at the wheel had stopped and taken her away. He told him the color of the vehicle and how long it took them to leave.

"But where? And why did they take her?"

"The Rasta boy was worried about the events that had occurred at the hands of the terrorist group."

"And now what am I going to tell my boss? They've kidnapped his protégée!" she exclaimed.

Hassna resisted her captors, but the two men were strong and held her down.

"What do you want? I'm not a tourist! I'm a Moroccan Arab like you," Hassna exclaimed desperately, screaming pitifully.

The men kept driving, continuing on their way without saying a word. They took her five kilometers from the place where they had kidnapped her. They were in the Erg Chebbi hamada, in an almost abandoned place. There were the Mifiss mines, the lead, quartz, and kohl mines, a material highly prized by the cosmetics industry long before they were exploited by the French.

Among the dunes and red sand, caravans of people riding dromedaries could be seen, and on the horizon the sunset showed its warm colors, but no one could imagine that Hassna was being kidnapped. They passed through a place full of herds of donkeys, palm trees, and golden dunes, a group of Berber nomadic dwellings and tents. The locals wore blue tunics and white turbans wrapped around their heads. They passed through green forests with farmland bathed by abundant rivers.

After a long journey, they arrived at the Mifiss mines. They parked the truck in front of an uninhabited, almost destroyed house. Two men were waiting there, looking like desert thieves. They had black mustaches and beards, were thin, and wore dark brown tunics and an Arab-style turban called a kafiyyeh.

They sat Hassna down, uncovered her sweaty face and tousled hair, and after searching the backpack Rasta Boy had given her, which contained provisions and water, they told her where the writings were, with sour and irascible expressions.

Hassna did not know what they were talking about. "There has been a mistake," she told them in a broken faltering voice. She was confused and disoriented by it all. She seemed dazed, but they ignored her. After mistreating her, threatening her, and pressuring her unsuccessfully, she remained completely confused. They decided to lock her in a two-by-two-meter room made of reddish mud, with a dirt floor and the smell of rotten goats.

The Rasta boy felt desperate because he didn't know where she was. The last hours of the day were falling on the city, and he asked his friend Said to take care of the girl until he returned if she showed up.

"I'm going out to look for help to find her."

Said promised he would.

Rasta Boy arrived at the luxurious tented camp just before nightfall, reporting the disappearance of a guest who had gone missing, or rather been kidnapped by two men in a dark green pickup truck. Hamid was in the office talking to his father, discussing the guests' departure due to the murders in the Imlil mountains and the cancellation of future stays. His father was very concerned that the business would go under due to the lack of tourists, which would cause an economic debacle.

When Hamid finished the meeting with his father, Rasta Boy was waiting outside to inform his boss so that he could report the kidnapping of the guest, Rania Nazer, to the police. Hamid overheard Rasta Boy's conversation with his father, intervened, and personally reported the kidnapping to the police. At that moment, the police were very busy investigating the murderers of the foreign women who had been killed. They gave him no hope that they would arrive soon, perhaps the next day, and told him that they would try to contact the Khamlia police to take charge.

Hamid gathered some men and went to the scene, in case anyone had seen anything more specific.

The police did not seem very interested, so they called for reinforcements from Fez, as reports had also been received of a theft of very old books.

A family in Mauritania treasured one of the finest collections of ancient Islamic manuscripts and valuable Koranic texts dating back to the 9th century. The books were bound in leather, paper, or parchment. They were kept in an old dusty library, which gave off the scent of a desert abbey declared a World Heritage Site by UNESCO. The books were so old that their pages looked like crumpled puff pastry; the ink was almost indelible, but they were extremely valuable. Of the 33,000 ancient texts, dating from the 10th century, 2,000 were in the National Museum.

In ancient times, the city of Chiguett, in Mauritania, in Saharan West Africa, was the city of librarians, a place where only 4,000 people lived, 5.20 km from its capital, Nouakchott.

Mauritania is a city protected by pale gold mountains, founded twelve centuries ago. The houses were built of reddish mud, with small windows and hand-carved doors. They were found in ruins, abandoned by their owners who fled the desert sands. One family remained there, amassing one of the finest collections of ancient Islamic manuscripts. In ancient times, it was one of the most visited places by caravans selling their goods, such as dates and salt, traveling from Marrakech to Fez carrying gold, slaves, and spices. It was a place where educated people came to rest in the oasis; others were scholars. The school director had seven hundred volumes in the collection.

The robbery took place in the school director's house and was perpetrated by men of Islamic origin. After assaulting him, they left him badly injured, tied up and gagged, and then stole the collection he kept in his home. It was nighttime and nothing could be done. They suspected that they would find a way to smuggle them into Morocco by taking them out in several volumes with different people, and then delivering them outside the country to a collector living in the desert of Marrakech.

Mauritania alerted Morocco to the possible entry of these valuable ancient volumes. The Moroccan police mobilized at the borders, resulting in a shortage of officers.

Marrakech is four hours away from Mauritania.

In 1960, Mauritania gained independence from France and is now part of the Islamic Republic of Mauritania.

By mistake, the men who had kidnapped Hassna confused her with the girl carrying a group of stolen volumes from the ancient collection. They saw her standing at the agreed time and place for the delivery and, as she was carrying a backpack, they thought she was the one.

Once the incident was cleared up, they had no intention of letting her go, as she could identify them and report them to the authorities, thus ruining the plan. While they decided what to do with her, she remained locked in the windowless adobe room, which also smelled like a bar bathroom and was stifling from the stench and heat. She heard someone securing the door with a tightly tied rope.

The green van returned to Khamlia, turned onto the same avenue, and stopped at the corner where the real girl was carrying a backpack. They lifted her into the van and sped off. One of the men held her tightly with the hands of a day laborer.

The bricklayer who was building a house wrote down the license plate number and the make, year and color of the vehicle.

When Hamid and Rasta Boy arrived with the boys, they went to the police station to look for the police, but only one could help them. The village bricklayer gave the information to Rasta Boy, and together with the boys, the police, and Hamid, they set off in search of the dark green truck.

"They can't be far away," argued the bricklayer.

"Where did they go?" asked Hamid.

"I think they headed for the abandoned mines," replied the bricklayer.

"Let's go," Hamid announced.

Hassna was crouched in a corner of the dirt floor, her head covered by her hijab. The dim moonlight filtered through the shack's flimsy roof. She heard someone unlocking and opening the door. It was one of the kidnappers. He threw her backpack to her so she could drink water and eat from her supplies. The hours seemed endless; she was alert to the movements outside: when they came in, when they went out, when they talked.

As the hours passed, she was struck by the silence outside. She drank some more water, but didn't eat anything. Everything she tried to eat was difficult to swallow. She looked around and saw a stone that protruded enough between the mud walls. With the help of her backpack buckle, she began to dig into the earth, holding it from the dry mud, which crumbled easily. Finally, she managed to get it out and hid it. Minutes later, she heard someone opening the door; it was the same man who had thrown her backpack at her. The man entered the room and, with an evil look on his face, stared at her and examined her. Hassna felt afraid; the man approached her and said:

"After this, no man will take you as his wife, and you will have to go and live with the prostitutes."

Hassna had protected her virginity like all Muslim girls of marriageable age. No man would forgive her dishonor, which would change her destiny abruptly and forever. She had to do something to protect her virginity. She thought of Rania and gathered her courage.

When the man lunged at her to grab her by force, an intense chill ran through her like a dagger, and in a rage, she grabbed the stone and struck him hard on the back of the neck, knocking him unconscious. She picked up her backpack very slowly and quietly and fled silently, terrified.

As evening fell, she walked through abandoned alleys and cobbled streets, listening to the echo of her footsteps between the empty doors. The ruined houses looked miserable; everything was destroyed, lonely, and desolate. She walked back and forth, knowing they would be looking for her. She continued through the dead streets without looking back, becoming aware of her unexpected reality and feeding her loneliness. She quickened her pace, attentive to the road, walking aimlessly through an empty place full of confusing shadows. She was afraid it would get darker. The streets were a succession of twists and turns, and she didn't know where she was or where to go. All she could think about was hiding in the ruins of a house. She had no intention of leaving that small abandoned village. Walking through the desert terrified her. She saw some African palm trees in the distance through the shadow of an inhospitable and threatening atmosphere, which showed an atmosphere of darkness filtering through the trees, staining them scarlet.

She slipped into the darkness, swallowing hard, and found herself hiding in a ruined house, crouching among bushes and collapsed adobe walls, stifling uncontrollable sobs, thinking that if she left, they might catch her and kidnap her again, and then yes, that man would abuse her. That night, she felt a pain and loneliness that gnawed at her insides with thoughts of a cruel end.

She waited for nightfall to begin walking in the darkness. She looked outside and the alley was quiet. She gathered her courage and decided to leave, as she felt a tightness in her chest where she was. She slipped away quietly into the darkness, moving slowly through a swirl of shadows, which she saw distorted. She wandered through the empty streets, her face covered, hiding her anguish and desolation. She continued quickly with a helpless and vague look, without looking back. The tops of the palm trees cast undulating shadows through which the wind whistled. It was a dark night; she was tired and couldn't organize her thoughts. She recognized her true situation, that no one knew where she was and that no one would help her. She thought again of Omar, of his comforting embrace when she was sad, but she was alone, wandering through unknown lands. Through her tears, she glimpsed the road as night fell and walked quickly despite being exhausted from the effort.

She remembered how, days before, she had gotten lost in the desert, walking almost to death among the sand and dunes, until her savior had arrived to bring her back to life.

And what good had it done her, if now she found herself once again in the clutches of a sinister fate?

She crossed dusty, rocky streets abandoned in ochre-colored ruins, which showed a succession of shadows and darkness. She walked as stealthily as possible, hiding her face in dark corners and nooks, stepping on puddles of water between narrow streets. The dim light gave her a terrifying appearance. She floated in the darkness like a drifting ship. The slow poison of fear began to run through her body as she walked, clutching her backpack with no water and few supplies. She was terrified at the thought of being found and returned to that gloomy, ghostly room. She was terrified of that man with tanned skin and red eyes who wanted to attack her. She couldn't get him out of her head. She walked along, biting her lips to keep from screaming or crying because of the nervousness that overwhelmed her. Tears ran down her veil, wetting the fabric and bringing back memories of the terrible, distressing hours in the desert. Until the faint moonlight guided her down an unknown path and she saw a dance of flickering shadows reflected on the cracked walls of abandoned houses, she continued to wander like a lost soul, until she finally emerged from the labyrinth and came to a wide, desolate, dark dirt road. She walked almost running, not knowing where to go. A faint light slowly spread, guiding her way; it was the glimmer of a star.

Hamid, along with the boys and Rasta Boy, accompanied by a guard, were heading for the kohl mines. They continued on their way and entered the highway that led to the abandoned city. Hamid thought anxiously of Hassna, left to fend for herself, remembering the warmth of those big dark eyes that shone with a special light that he had not been able to erase from his mind.

Suddenly, they saw someone wandering along the side of the road in the distance. Hamid approached very slowly, pulling the truck over to the side of the road. As he got closer, he realized it was Hassna. His heart leapt with joy. When she saw the vehicle , she panicked. Then, upon hearing her name, Hamid's face appeared and the darkness around her came to life with the light from the vehicle's headlights. He looked at her silently, his face tired and haggard, and found a small, wounded lioness who remained defensive. He walked slowly toward her and embraced her, asking,

"Are you okay, Rania?"

She nodded, bursting into tears of joy, and a smile lit up the darkness. Hamid helped her into the truck, caressing the smooth metal of her eyes with his gaze. Hassna showed him the place where she had been kidnapped. As he hugged her, he felt her thin body tremble with fear for the second time.

The police and the men arrived and quickly searched the place, arresting the thieves, the ringleader, and the collector of the oldest

Koran manuscripts. They also found valuable objects and stolen works of art. They had their hideout and operations in this almost uninhabited place. They recovered the ancient collection of manuscripts, which were returned to the museum and their owners in the city of Mauritania.

Hamid set off on his way back to the luxury shops. Hassna thanked Hamid again.

"Please accept my invitation to dinner," she said. "Your SUV is parked near your shop and your suitcase with your clothes is in your room. I'll wait for you. I'll come and pick you up at nine."

Hassna accepted, thanked him for the invitation, and retired to her tent to bathe and prepare for the date. She felt exhausted, not only physically but also psychologically; a lot had happened that day. She felt safe again. She felt calm after seeing Hamid, her savior, again. She thought about Omar again, who had somehow sensed her presence and her promise to always take care of her.

"I see everything differently now. I feel a powerful hand protecting me. Omar, where are you, my dear friend, my lifelong companion? Why did you leave and abandon me? Perhaps you are here and I cannot see you. You take care of me and protect me."

She took a bath to relax her tired body, then lay down on the bed and fell asleep for a while.

She woke up with a start, thinking that what had happened was a nightmare, but then she realized the truth.

Hassna took out some purchases she had made in the medina from her small suitcase: a beautiful veil that matched a pink gauze tunic with white embroidery on the collar and cuffs, which highlighted the color of her black eyes.

Given the time of the meeting, dinner came as an enchanted elixir. Hamid appeared in Hassna's shop wearing a blue tunic with yellow trim on the collar and cuffs, and a blue turban on his head.

He knocked on the door of Hassna's tent and she came out to greet him with a heavenly smile. He was amazed by her beauty, so different from other days when he had seen her almost dying. The impact of seeing her so beautiful was so great that he couldn't stop stealing glances at her, and the sparkle in her eyes unsettled him, making him feel that his life was threatened by a great fire of love.

They walked to the dining tent in silence, so impressed by each other.

When they reached the dining room, they gazed at the shining sphere smiling down at them from the heavens. They entered their private room, lit by candle, whose light caressed their silhouettes. They sat barefoot on the carpets. Rasta Boy arrived to take their order. They ordered beef tagine with apples and raisins, fish with almonds and pistachios. While their food was being served, they drank mint tea accompanied by honey and sesame cookies.

Hassna asked Hamid if he was also staying there and if he was on vacation like her. Hamid replied that yes, he was on vacation and that he lived in Spain, where he practiced law.

"And what are you doing alone in the desert, apart from getting lost?" Hamid asked.

They smiled.

She replied, "It's a long and painful story that I'd rather not remember right now."

He said, "When you're ready and want to tell me, I'll be waiting."

Hassna began with a sigh: "Many years ago, I lived in Malaga with my family. When my parents died in a plane crash five years ago, I was sent to Granada to stay with my father's brother and his wife. I was a boarder at a school until I finished high school."

She lowered her head, overcome with emotion, and refused to continue talking. He realized that she had become sad and changed the subject. Hassna thanked him for his understanding and patience, and they talked about the place and how beautiful the desert was.

Rasta Boy arrived with dinner, placed it in the middle of a small table, and they shared the dishes, eating with their right hands. After dinner, they went outside the tent for a walk.

The moon's halo had taken over the sky, providing absolute clarity to appreciate it in all its splendor. They climbed the dunes in the moonlight, Hamid holding her hand. Hassna's body trembled with pleasure and a shower of shivers washed over her waist. Hassna felt a pleasant flutter of butterflies as she felt his large, strong hand merge with hers under the starry sky, causing a sharp sensation in her stomach. She shivered at the splendid sight of the night, and her warm hands went weak. He looked at her, and the embarrassed blush on her cheeks spread to the roots of her hair. That night seemed wonderful to her as she breathed deeply, saturated with love and moonlight. Then they slowly began their journey back, the starlight fading along the way.

They descended from the summit, Hassna helped by Hamid as her feet sank up to her calves in the fine sand. They remained there appreciating the peace and tranquility of the Sahara until the distant sound of drums and Berber music interrupted the silence. They returned to the tents and sat around a large bonfire, where the shadows of the flames danced nervously to the sound of the night band playing and singing in the company of the vacationing guests.

Every time Hamid called her Rania, Hassna wanted to tell him that this was not her first name, and that Nazer was her surname, but she feared that this would complicate matters. She had still not heard from Rania or her uncle.

The idea of leaving the Sahara seemed daunting to her. There, for the moment, she felt safe and unnoticed in Hamid's company. She was rediscovering the joy of being happy again because, although she didn't admit it to herself, love was creeping into her heart and she was quietly entering into the fullness of a new life.

They spent a pleasant evening together, Hamid accompanied her to her tent, and they agreed to go camel riding the next day. Hassna accepted. He watched her calmly, holding his breath, for his indifference was nothing more than a shield against fear.

Hamid moved to the tent next door, as it was empty that night and neither of them could sleep. The stars filtered through a hole in his tent and smiled at him with the sparkle in their eyes. Hamid thought of Hassna and her splendid fleeting, innocent face, which he found moving, and at the same time of her attractive, delicate body with the seductive curves of a woman, sleeping a few meters away from him.

Once in the tent, Hassna released all the tension of the last few days. She thought that at dawn she would tell Hamid the whole truth and that perhaps after that a sad fate awaited her, since, upon arriving in the desert, she had distanced herself from her troubled and confusing reality, which weighed on her shoulders more than a guilty conscience.

Hassna, despite not knowing Hamid, inspired confidence in him and showed great integrity. She felt protected. All she knew about him was that he was a lawyer, that he lived in Spain, and that he was on vacation. He, for his part, knew nothing about her, only a little about her past life, and not even her real name, which made her feel guilty without being so. She felt she was betraying the person who cared so much about her and had even gone to the trouble of providing her with a cell phone with coverage to communicate with Spain. That man was golden.

The next morning, Hassna called Rania's phone. She answered:

"I finally have news from you!"

Hassna was very happy to hear her friend's voice.

"How are things in Granada?"

"I'll tell you that your uncle is in jail for the murder of your aunt Lalla!"

"Aunt Lalla is dead?"

Hassna felt a chill run down her spine, her mouth went dry, and she froze, unable to utter a word to ask the question.

"Your uncle killed her because she wouldn't reveal where you were."

Hassna sobbed, feeling her legs tremble.

"Poor aunt, she'll be with Allah now," Hassna said between stifled gasps.

"She was also accused of stealing money from one of your companies to finance her nights of gambling in underground clubs. She was also accused of kidnapping you and confining you to the sanatorium, which, incidentally was closed and both the doctors and nurses were imprisoned."

Hassna told Rania all about her terrible experience in the desert and how she had finally been rescued by a boy who saved her in the desert.

"Hassna, my dear friend," added Rania, "I'll be with you this weekend."

"I'm so happy, Rania! You don't know how long I've waited for this moment and to be together again!"

Hassna asked Rania to collect her clothes, passport, and credit cards from Manssur's house before traveling to the desert and bring them to her so she could return to Spain with her own passport.

"I'll be with you, Hassna, this weekend."

"Thank you, my friend, and thank you to your father. I'll have the opportunity to thank him personally when we return."

They said goodbye on the phone, very happy that everything had worked out. Hassna was free to return to Spain.

The next day, Hamid showed up with two dromedaries for a ride after breakfast. The day was sunny and the sky was clear. They had breakfast together in the dining tent, served by Rasta Boy.

Hassna's face was lit up with happiness, her body relaxed as she enjoyed Hamid's company and the imminent arrival of Rania.

After breakfast, he helped Hassna mount the dromedario and they set off on their journey across the golden sands of the Sahara desert. They rode side by side, leaving tracks along the silent path, taking in the immensity of the desert. There was nothing on the horizon, just them in that golden sea that stretched to infinity. The sunlight barely shone. Hassna smiled and he looked at her. They didn't need to speak to know how they felt about each other; the voracity of the bonfire of their lives was threatened by a great fire of love.

"Where are we going?" Hassna asked.

"For now, we'll ride through the desert and the dunes, but I'd like to take a longer ride another day so you can see some interesting places before we get to Marrakech. I'd like to take you horseback riding along the Atlantic coast, reach the coastal dunes, and soak up the sun."

She smiled and nodded.

They traveled a long way and arrived at a palm grove, where there was a nomad tent nearby. They approached, dismounted, and entered the small tent, sitting barefoot on the small rug. They were treated with hospitality and welcomed with the usual mint tea, dates, and almond sweets. They savored the tea, rested, and then set off on their return journey. They both fell in love, but it was not appropriate for Hamid to kiss Hassna, as in Muslim culture it was considered an assault on modesty. If Hamid wanted to kiss Hassna, he would first have to marry her, and she knew it. That's why they walked and talked to get to know each other better. Then, on the day of the engagement, he would be introduced to the bride's parents, but not before. In Hassna's case, she had no family to introduce; a wali would have to give his consent.

On the way back, they were both very happy to have shared such beautiful and magical moments together, and suddenly, a blue and purple gap appeared in the sky, harmonizing with the bright colors of the rainbow.

Hassna's heart sank as she thought about how the man who had saved her life twice knew nothing about her. I'll have to tell him everything before Rania arrives, she thought.

"But how would he take it? Would he feel betrayed that I had deceived him with a name that wasn't mine? Maybe he won't want to see me again. What if I lose him forever?" These questions tormented Hassna.

She was attracted to Hamid. It had been almost nine months since Omar's death, and her wounds had begun to heal after meeting Hamid, whose name in Arabic means "worthy of praise."

Hamid was ten years older than Hassna, but she liked him and felt happy with him, although she was also aware that he was only passing through , that his life was in Madrid, and that it was better not to get her hopes up about a holiday romance.

That night, Hamid in his tent, searched his computer for a private plane crash that had occurred five years earlier in Malaga. When he found the news on the front page, he felt confused because the surnames did not match. He was shocked. It couldn't be possible, since their surnames were different: Azzim and Izza Sabal Saadi.

"A successful business magnate dies alongside his wife when their private jet crashes on landing at Malaga airport. They leave behind an eleven-year-old daughter, the sole heir to the Sabal Saadi empire."

"Everything matches except the surname. Is it a coincidence? Has she changed her surname? Has she run away and is on the run?" thought Hamid. "What could have happened to her to make her so sad when she talks about it?"

That night, Hamid couldn't sleep, wondering what secret the young woman was keeping as she traveled alone through the desert. He also thought about how to tell her or ask her about what he thought he had discovered.

"If it's a coincidence, I'd be embarrassed that I've been investigating her. I'd better wait for her to tell me."

A winding road awaited Hassna at dawn. She headed early to the dining tent to start the day with borji, dates, and coconut sweets. Rasta Boy greeted her respectfully and asked her what she would like for breakfast. She replied that she would like to go and serve herself breakfast from the buffet.

That morning, Hassna did not see Hamid in the dining room, as he usually arrived early for breakfast.

The morning passed slowly, and her mind was immersed in the difficult adventure that awaited her: telling Hamid the whole truth, no matter what happened.

She returned to his shop and saw that it was locked from the outside.

"Where could he have gone?" she wondered.

She sat attentively outside the shop, on benches covered with rugs that covered the sand, hoping to see Hamid.

The sun's rays appeared discreetly, further crystallizing the clarity of the golden morning. Under a suddenly clear sky, the landscape shone with splendid clarity, revealing a cheerful and peaceful morning. In the distance, she saw a caravan of bedouins on dromedaries, one after another, dressed in white robes and turbans, showing the way to a group of visitors.

The Rasta boy passed by and she asked him if he had seen Hamid. He told her that Hamid was in the office with his father.

"Has Hamid's father arrived in the desert?" Hassna asked.

"He lives here, miss, he owns the luxury shops and the Arabian horse stud farm."

Hassna was thoughtful; Hamid hadn't said anything about it.

That morning, Rania called Hassna on her cell phone.

"Friend, I'm at Manssur's house looking for your passport."

Hassna told her where it was, along with her credit cards.

"I'll be traveling soon to meet up with you."

"Come soon, Rania. Now that everything is over, let's go for a walk and get to know Morocco."

"Hassna, you must come back soon to claim your inheritance and testify before the judge about the abuse you suffered at the sanatorium at the hands of the doctors and nurses, so that the judge can pass sentence."

"It will be later, Rania, when we get back. The signal is bad here, I can't hear you very well. See you tomorrow."

"Okay, friend, take care, see you soon, bye."

Hassna was deeply saddened by the death of aunt Lalla, who had sacrificed her life to save her, and she thought again: now she will be enjoying herself in the kingdom of Allah.

"With my uncle in prison," she thought, "my long days of sadness are finally over. Allah, your mighty hand has saved me from death. I feel safe. Should I feel this way? I see everything differently and clearly. But I have something difficult to confess to Hamid."

At sunset, Hamid appeared. Hassna saw him and they greeted each other. They walked together to their tents and Hamid told her that she had to wash and change her clothes for dinner.

"Would you like to have dinner together?" Hamid asked.

Hassna gladly accepted.

"How about eight o'clock?"

"I'll wait for you," Hassna replied.

As Hamid retired to his tent, Hassna thought about getting ready and how she would tell Hamid that her name was not Rania, but , and that she was waiting for the real Rania, a friend who was coming on vacation to explore beyond Merzouga and end the trip in Marrakech before returning to Granada.

She had to clarify her situation, especially regarding her name. She didn't want him to see her as a liar and an impostor.

Hamid thought that perhaps Hassna would tell him the rest of her story that night. From Rasta Boy, he had learned that Hassna knew her father lived there and owned the luxury shops. He would have liked to tell her, but introducing her to his father so soon without knowing her well didn't seem appropriate, even though he was crazy about her.

It was dinner time, and Hamid went to find Hassna. She was very happy to see him. They both looked very handsome and went to the dining room, where they sat in their usual place.

The dim candlelight flickered, creating the impression that they were dancing. They sat barefoot on cushions placed on beautiful rugs to enjoy Moroccan dishes. They ordered charcoal-grilled lamb and a salad with hazelnuts, almonds, vegetables, peppers, zucchini, meats, and cilantro as the main ingredient.

Silence fell between them until Hamid started the conversation, telling Hassna that he had been at his father's stud farm early that morning, helping to select horses for sale.

"That's why I hadn't seen you all day," Hassna replied. "Your father lives here, doesn't he?" Hassna asked, even though she already knew.

He nodded and told her that his father owned the luxurious tent hotel.

"And your mother?" Hassna asked.

"She passed away six years ago."

"I'm sorry," she replied. "Do you have any siblings?"

"I have an older brother who is married, a lawyer, and lives in Madrid. What about you?" asked Hamid, very interested.

Hassna hesitated and began to tell him from the beginning how she was at her father's partner's house and received the bitter news of her parents' accident, and was transferred to Granada to live with her uncle and his wife Lalla, then the death of her fiancé on the eve of their wedding; her confinement in the psychiatric center and her escape with the help of Rania and her aunt, Lalla; her change of identity to escape her uncle and save her life, the adventure of choosing the desert to hide, and also the terrifying story of the foreign girls murdered in the mountains of Imlil.

During dinner, at which they were the only diners, she told him in detail the sad story of her life.

"My real name is Hassna Sabal Saadi..."

Hamid, seeing her speak and become emotional, her eyes filled with tears as she told her story, advised her to cry as much as she wanted without feeling ashamed, as nothing was better than tears to bring relief. She needed to unburden her soul and free herself, and her tears flowed into his heart. He had a lump in his throat that prevented him from swallowing the anguish of thinking how much that poor, brave young girl had suffered in facing those situations.

"You already know what happened next," Hassna added, "you saved my life twice from the clutches of death."

Hamid listened to her with great emotion, took her hands and held them tenderly, kissing her with his eyes as if he wanted her to feel that she was not alone. Then he changed the subject, looked at her and said:

"Hassna, I like your name. It means 'beautiful' in Arabic, and it suits you very well."

Hassna smiled and felt a great relief in her soul as she unloaded the inner heaviness that was burning inside her. She was glad that not a single cloud clouded the dream union she had created in her mind, toward the force of love that burned in her chest, a love that not even a million firefighters could extinguish.

She smiled, and he wiped away the tears that had fallen down her cheeks.

Hassna thought about how much he resembled Omar: so sensitive, affectionate, and concerned for her. She remembered when she got lost, wandering through the desert, fainting and feeling death looming over her, and she cried out, "Omar, where are you?" before losing consciousness. Then she appeared in that nomad tent, saved by Hamid.

"Did Allah send him to help me?" she wondered.

"If it weren't for the fact that the Koran rejects the belief in reincarnation, I would think it was Omar or that Allah had sent Hamid to take care of me. When I met him, it was as if the sun had come out after all those dark months of suffering. I found in him the remedy for my misfortune."

Hamid told Hassna that he would soon return to Spain, to Madrid, to work at the law firm.

"I hope we can continue to see each other. I'll give you my phone number so you have it if you need my help."

She wrote it down on her cell phone, as he didn't have any business cards.

Hassna thanked him and they had dinner together, happy to have cleared up both situations. That night, they both felt sad because the vacation was over and each would go their separate ways.

Very early in the morning, the sun was rising, a beautiful golden tapestry over the desert and the real Rania arrived at the camp, brought by one of the vans from the luxurious tented hotel.

Rasta Boy took her belongings to Hassna's tent, went inside and found Hassna just waking up. The girls hugged each other warmly, kissed each other once on one cheek and five times on the other, according to Moroccan custom, and jumped and skipped with joy. They sat on the bed and chatted for a long time until after noon, telling each other everything that had happened.

"Poor Aunt Lalla," Hassna said, "so sweet and loving. She must be in Allah's kingdom now. She died because she didn't betray me. What a pity..." She bowed her head and shed a few tears.

"Aunt Lalla left me a letter that served as evidence to imprison Manssur for the murder of your aunt. She said that since your uncle had no children, you, Hassna, were the heir to his house, and that was all, since your uncle's company went bankrupt due to his gambling addiction. Thank goodness your inheritance was saved in time. You have to testify before the judge. Dad will let us know the date of the hearing. Let's forget this period of misfortune," Rania announced to cheer Hassna up. She showed her the clothes she had brought from her wardrobe.

"I brought veils, tunics, underwear, and, look at this, our dance dresses."

"Thank you!" exclaimed Hassna, "but I don't know where we can dance, even though I love it."

"Here, Hassna!" exclaimed Rania, "in this store, just like in the old days. Do you remember when we used to dance in the bedroom practicing for the recital? I can download music on my cell phone."

"Deal!"

They put on beaded belly dancing outfits, Hassna showing off her beautiful black hair and a yellow two-piece sequined dance costume. The silk veil gave her an ethereal air, barefoot, with gold anklets and a bracelet that connected her wrist to a chain that ran down to her middle finger and ended in a ring. She wore large hoop earrings.

Rania wore a jade green dress; both looked beautiful. It was noon and they had no idea what time it was as they discussed memories amid tears of laughter. Hassna put on the music and they began to dance. The room was quite spacious and proved to be a good setting for dancing. They were transported back a year, dancing like in the old days.

The music seeped through the seams of the tent canvas, releasing the melody like the scent of a sensual woman. Hamid arrived to welcome Rania, as he had not had the opportunity to meet her. He stopped when he heard the music and knocked on the tent door, but they were so absorbed in dancing that they didn't hear him. Hamid peeked through a half-open crack and was so impressed that his bushy eyebrows arched into a smile when he saw Hassna in all her splendor. Her long, slightly wavy hair was uncovered, her slender body perfect and sensual, her movements in time with the swaying of her veil, the exciting sway of her firm, shapely hips shaking beneath the veil, and the sound of the dangling coins that fluttered from her waist, the voluptuous curves of her hips and her warm golden thighs escaping from under the transparent fabric of her skirt. Her lush, firm, voluptuous young breasts were driving him crazy.

He watched the dance, feeling chills, paralyzed by love; he felt his manhood aroused by passion, trapped under his white tunic.

Then they played more music and Hassna placed a saber on her head, making smooth, undulating movements with her hips, demonstrating sensuality, freedom, appreciating the harmony and subtlety in the dance, while balancing the saber on her head.

Rania began her next dance with fans that relieved stress when they touched her chakra. The veil covered her and revealed her transparency when she wanted it to.

Suddenly, the Rasta boy interrupted Hamid's spell to ask him if they were going to have lunch. Hamid covered his mouth and gestured for him to be quiet, not letting him see the girls dancing. He ordered him to go to the dining room and set the table for three people.

After the dance, Hamid called the tent. Hassna told him they would be out in a few minutes. The girls waited a moment to open the tent while he listened fortuitously to the golden sound of their laughter as they quickly changed their hijabs. The tent flap opened as Hamid sat outside on a bench, appreciating the dawn light that drew amber curls on the horizon over the golden sands of the desert.

Hassna introduced him to her friend Rania, and they chatted for a while as the desert offered them a magnificent spectacle that Rania had never seen before. The three of them walked to the dining tent under the scorching midday sun to enjoy a delicious lunch.

Rania told Hamid that her father was also a lawyer and that he was handling Hassna and her uncle's case. They became good friends since they had both saved Hassna from death.

The sun gave way to the moon, which pierced through the curtains of floating clouds and glimpsed the clarity radiating its light with joy. When night fell, the three of them had dinner, sharing their delicious food and musical evenings under the desert stars and the moon, whose light filtered faintly through the palm leaves to the sound of Berber music played by the band around the bonfire. Rania, also a descendant of Berber parents, was happy to share the songs with her friends. They talked a lot, sharing anecdotes and memories.

"Hassna," he announced, "today you are among your three saviors and protectors, including Allah." She smiled, cherishing her newfound happiness. They said goodbye at sunset after the Berber concert, as the moon rose in the sky that night.

Three days had passed and the day of farewell had arrived. He had to leave for Madrid. Hamid respectfully embraced Hassna, feeling his heart beat with love. He looked her in the eyes and said:

"I hope to see you soon."

Hassna felt the pulse of her free will in her blood, but the love she felt for him was nothing more than fleeting images. A sharp clarity of nostalgia took hold of her, having left behind forever the darkness stalked by the caress of the moon in the desert, a fleeting ray of sunshine that hid her longing for farewell deep in her chest.

Hamid looked at Rania and said, "Take good care of her."

Hassna replied, "Shuk ran Hamid."

They watched him drive away in the truck, leaving a trail of smoke and dust in his wake on the road.

Rania noticed Hassna's sad face and cheered her up.

"Let's plan our trip."

Hassna perked up.

"I have the 4x4 truck," she said, "I rented it for three months in your name, the term expires in a week, we'll have to extend it for two more weeks."

"Hassna, I brought you your passport, your credit cards, and everything else," Rania announced.

"Thank you, my friend, for everything you've done for me, helping me and putting yourself out there. I'll deposit the amount of all my expenses, including my travel expenses and yours, into your bank account. Your friendship is priceless."

"Thank you, my friend," replied Rania, and they hugged. "It's been a pleasure to help you, Hassna."

They prepared for the next day's journey. Rasta Boy had equipped the 4x4 truck with enough gasoline, water, and supplies, following Hamid's orders. Hassna thanked him for all his kindness, took a photo with him, and they set off for Rissani.

They felt very comfortable and happy to be traveling together after so many months without seeing each other. A lot had happened, and they would have 42 km to talk about it before reaching Rissani. Hassna would have exactly 44 minutes to open up and tell Rania how she felt about Hamid during those days they had shared together.

Rania realized that there was a certain attraction between them. She wanted to ask her if there had been anything more than friendship. She didn't want to be nosy or intrusive, but she needed to know why her friend's eyes had lost the sparkle they had two days before Hamid left. Rania knew Hassna as if she were her sister and didn't want to see her suffer again. She gathered all her courage and asked her:

"Hassna, how do you feel about Hamid?"

Hassna stopped the truck, looked at Rania, and replied:

"Why are you asking me that? He's just a friend. We met at a very opportune moment, as he saved my life, that's all."

The indifference she showed towards him was nothing more than an escape route to hide the torment of her love; the desire to forget him and get him out of her mind was a stronger incentive to remember him, and the more she thought about him, the angrier she became.

"It seemed to me that he liked you. I saw how he looked at you all the time and tried to take care of you. Look at the truck," she ordered the Rasta boy to equip it with everything necessary for the trip, "the only thing missing was for him to lend us a companion to take care of us."

Hassna smiled and said to Rania,

"I had noticed, but I didn't want to get my hopes up, since it was just a holiday friendship. He must have his own life in Spain, and I have to make decisions that I'm not ready for yet. When I get there, I'll have to start studying so I can understand how to manage the companies my father left me. Although there are qualified people to continue running them successfully, I wouldn't want to appear ignorant at a board meeting. I wouldn't want to be distracted from my goal by courtship or marriage.

"If that's how you feel, that's fine, but from what I saw, he would be a good match. He's a lawyer, cultured, handsome, and single."

Hassna looked at Rania, puzzled.

"And now you want me to get married? When I was going to marry Omar, you discouraged me and didn't agree."

"That's true, Hassna, but what you felt for Omar wasn't love, just a childhood friendship. You'll see that when the day comes, you'll agree with me."

Hassna didn't respond. She didn't want to accept it, but for her, meeting Hamid had been something special. She had felt things she had never felt for Omar.

"Could it be love that I feel?" she wondered.

"I'm afraid of love and running away from happiness. My heart has suffered a lot. It terrifies me and prevents me from giving it away again and getting hurt. Am I doomed never to love? Time heals, it makes you forget. I resist loving, but I can't get it out of my head. It disturbs my body and disturbs my soul. I was wandering in the desert and you found an oasis for me. Why am I looking for excuses to forget him? But the more I forget him, the more I think about him. Is loving the same as being happy? My soul was downcast, sad, and overwhelmed without love before I met him."

The moment he left, Hassna felt a deep pain in the depths of her soul, but she didn't want to accept it, nor did she want to know how to get him out of her mind, as he had given her proof of knowing the other side of the moon, and the trail of memory knew no bounds.

She changed the subject, and Rania realized she was right; she knew her friend too well to realize that she was struggling internally to accept that she was in love with Hamid.

The clouds traveled quickly, shaped like white cotton. They entered the city of Rissani, in the province of Errachidia, located near Erfoud. It was a large city almost comparable to Erg Chebbi, the largest desert in Morocco in the High Atlas. Hamid's absence weighed on her like an oppressive shadow. When she thought she might never see him again, she kept that beautiful memory in her heart and in the hard drive of her memory.

They traveled along magnificent roads, passing red buildings and structures, and entered the city through a large Moorish-style arch with three red flags and a star in the center. Along the way, the mosques, old commercial buildings, and multitude of cars and bicycles surprised Rania.

They entered the most authentic market in southern Morocco. The sun's rays illuminated the streets of the labyrinthine medina, and a beam of diffused light fell vertically on them. The neighing and braying of the animals being sold in the souk could be heard. There were mules, oxen, and the bustle of people in front of the animals was like a buzzing in their ears. They found the largest donkey market and the nomads who had come to the market to stock up and sell goats, cows, and sheep. Numerous merchants could be seen passing by.

They entered the market on foot, where spices were sold, and the scene displayed a rainbow of bright colors. They strolled around and bought fruit to continue their journey. On their way out, they came across a group of musicians sitting on a carpet, dressed in white robes and orange turbans like a large crown over their black hair that shone like wet stones, playing drums, flutes, and guitars, and singing songs of the desert.

They continued along the road and arrived at the Draa Valley, a picturesque place full of date palms, lush vegetation, and the mighty Draa River, the largest in Morocco.

Along the way, they ate dates and fruit they had bought at the market. Rasta Boy had provided them with fresh coconut water to drink. Hassna, although enjoying the trip, couldn't stop thinking about Hamid; it bothered her greatly, even more than Rania had noticed.

"What or who are you thinking about?" Rania asked, knowing the answer.

"Nothing; I'm just appreciating this beautiful, simple, peaceful place, far from the hustle and bustle of the world, from worries and problems," Hassna replied, not wanting to accept what Rania was thinking, and she was right.

They arrived at the Troda Gorge, a famous canyon with gloomy vaults and immense mountains where people came to climb. It was a deep ravine located in the High Atlas, in the valley of the Dades River, the longest in Morocco and Algeria. They began a twenty-four-kilometer descent along a winding road toward the Troda Gorge, revealing an impressive alley of vertical walls that rose toward the sky between several rugged mountains three hundred meters high, with shapes and folds of Mesozoic erosive materials and fossils in the stones.

During the descent, Rania felt ill and they had to stop for a few minutes until she recovered and returned after vomiting. There were a few more curves ahead and they came across palm trees, farmland, and adobe villages called kasbahs.

Finally, they reached the bottom of the gorge, a plain where the waters of the river mingled in the distance, watering a charming palm grove where crystal-clear springs flowed. There were some children playing and bathing in the river, which formed a large natural pool.

Rania took the opportunity to go into the river, taking off her shoes to drink fresh water and wash her face and hands a little. It was a hot day, and you could smell the coolness of the river and hear the insects fluttering over the leaves of the bushes swaying in the silent wind.

They got back into the truck and parked next to a hotel.

They got out of the 4x4 and walked towards a beautiful palm grove, whose green color contrasted with the orange earth and the spectacular sky that morning under the scorching sun.

They spotted the hotel, built into the rock of the mountain. As they entered, they could hear the sweet sound of the cool, crystal-clear river water and the croaking of frogs jumping on a green blanket of leaves floating in the water.

As she got out of the truck, Rania tripped over a rock and twisted her ankle, and would have fallen if it hadn't been for Hassna, who bent down to help her. In turn, Rania saved Hassna's life again when they felt the impact of a bullet that grazed her head.

The hitman, after searching for a long time in various places, found her and her friend.

Realizing that their lives were in danger, the girls quickly entered the hotel and asked if there were any rooms available. Unfortunately, it was full of tourists and they had no reservations. They went to the hotel shop that sold souvenirs, clothes, and other items of interest, and bought a couple of tunics and veils of different colors from . They went to the bathroom and changed their appearance. Hassna even padded her stomach to look pregnant so she could leave the hotel unnoticed and begin her journey.

They quietly left the hotel alongside a couple who were also leaving, while others sat on the terrace by the river drinking mint tea with date paste and admiring the stunning beauty of the architecture.

When the girls reached their van, the hitman recognized them by their vehicle and tried to point his gun at them again, but the sound of his cell phone interrupted his maneuver. It was the detective, warning the hitman to abort the plan. "Don't kill the girl, let her go and come back."

Hassna and Rania, very frightened quickly fled the scene, sensing that the danger had not ended with Manssur's arrest, and continued their journey. Along the way, they realized that no one was following them; they thought that perhaps it had been a coincidence.

Rania's sprained ankle was getting better and they continued their journey to the Dades Valley, dodging donkeys, cows, goats, and sheep along the way. Along the way, they saw trees and small villages, and came across palm trees laden with dates and people harvesting them.

Granada

Manssur in prison, was surprised by an unexpected visit when he was told that someone was coming to see him.

"Who could be visiting me?" he wondered.

If he had known who it was, he would not have gone out. It was Idir, a mafia gambler to whom he owed five hundred thousand euros in bets.

"I'm in jail, Idir, I have no way to pay you back."

"Think about how you'll do it. I have friends in prison who can remind you of the debt."

Manssur was worried and scared; he had no money to pay Idir. A few days later, Idir came back to visit him and pressured him to pay his debt. On his way to his cell, Manssur first went to the bathroom, where two inmates were waiting for him and beat him so badly that he ended up in the infirmary. Two days later, Idir came to the prison looking for an answer.

Manssur came out with his face disfigured and swollen.

"Please Idir, don't hit me anymore, I'll pay you with my house, but you'll have to wait for my lawyer to put it up for sale."

"No way, Manssur. I've waited too long. Pay up if you don't want my friends to give you another reminder. Call your lawyer and transfer your property to me. I'll give you five days."

"Idir, my property is worth much more than the debt."

"I'm sorry, I can't wait months for time to pass and for it not to sell. Five days, or another reminder."

Manssur, mortified, asked to see his lawyer to put his residence in Granada in Idir's name. He had nothing left; he had lost everything, even his freedom. That was his punishment.

Madrid

Hamid arrived at his law firm after his vacation in the desert and found his brother Hassan happy with the news that he would soon be a father. Hamid congratulated him very familiarly with a big hug and a kiss on each cheek in the Spanish style, since Muslim men greet each other by placing their right hand on their chest.

"Tell me, brother, how is Dad and his business?" Hassan asked.

"My father is in very good health, but he is concerned about the terrorist attacks that are scaring away tourists and have significantly reduced his business. I have been helping him sell the thoroughbred horses, but he is worried about the future of Las Jaimas de Lujo."

"Poor father, his life is the desert; he should retire and come to live in Madrid, but you know how stubborn he is, and taking him away from there would be the death of him. But he's not the only one who's worried; our king, Mohammed VI, is also concerned about the decline in tourism. He has been building roads, hotels, and hostels to accommodate visitors for some time now, which is a significant investment for our country. But tell me about you, brother. Haven't you chosen a bride to marry yet? You're old enough to start a family, so I'm going to make you an uncle!"

Hamid smiled.

"Patience, brother, maybe I'll find the woman of my life soon."

Hamid retired to his office thinking about Hassna, wondering what had become of her, and the lack of news had him worried. "I hope she remembers me, poor girl, with everything she's been through."

The internal bell in his office rang. It was his secretary.

"Good morning, Layla, how can I help you?"

"It's Miss Titrit. I told her you've just returned from a trip, but she insists on seeing you. If you like, I can arrange an appointment for another day."

"All right, Layla, send her in."

Titrit entered Hamid's office.

She looked spectacular, with a graceful gait that made her appear interesting and elegant. She was twenty three years old, tall and slim, with cherry-colored skin, large eyes, thick, dreamy eyelashes, and full lips. She was a very sweet girl with a contagious joy.

"How are you, Titrit?" Hamid announced, appreciating her beauty.

"Very well, Hamid. And you, when did you arrive?"

"I arrived yesterday morning. How can I help you?"

"Well, I'd like to buy a property that's for sale on Paseo del General Martínez, and I'd like your advice. Since you have notaries here, they could take care of all the legal paperwork."

"All right, Titrit; at your service; we are here to serve you."

"Thank you, Hamid. With all this, I haven't asked you about your father."

"I just got back from the desert. I went to see my father. The poor man is struggling with his 'luxury shops' business, as he is very concerned about the recent terrorist attacks that are scaring away tourists. But he keeps himself busy. He also has the stud farm, which brings in a good income."

"He shouldn't be working anymore and should devote himself to traveling," Titrit insisted.

"But there's no way he'll listen to me. He says he'd get bored and doesn't like traveling alone. Since Mom died, he's thrown himself into his work. I hope that when Hassan's son is born, he'll come to Madrid more often and delegate the business."

"Hassan is going to have a child? How wonderful! What about you, Hamid? When are you going to get a girlfriend? It's about time."

Hamid smiled and replied.

"Everyone wants me to get married, but be patient, everything in its own time."

"Rachid sends his best wishes. He couldn't come because he had a doctor's appointment. Next time he'll be here to start the process of buying the property. Goodbye Hamid, I know you're very busy, I won't keep you any longer. Thank you very much (shukran bezaf)."

"Goodbye, Titrit, it was good to see you. Say hello to Rachid."

Layla, the secretary, entered Hamid's office and apologized for disturbing him with the girl's visit.

Hamid explained that Titrit was very dear to the family and that whenever she came by, she could let her in, as long as he wasn't with a client.

Layla was satisfied and returned to her office.

Desert

The girls crossed the Dades Valley, admiring its frenetic adobe constructions, the herds of dromedaries with their owners dressed in white tunics and orange turbans, walking among palm trees and bushes called tamaris (food for dromedaries), which contrasted with the bright green color of the valley.

They entered the Ziz Valley, the city of four square towers intended to be the residences of powerful people. At Rania's insistence, they went down to the donkey medina where they were all parked for sale. She fell in love with a little white donkey with droopy ears and insisted on buying it. Hassna convinced her not to because, even though the donkey was very small, no matter how hard they pushed it, it would not fit in the truck, and pulling it with the 4x4 would make the trip very slow.

"It will also be a problem during the trip," Hassna said.

Rania was very sad. They walked to the medina market to buy spices, pastries, cheese, and honey. They continued their journey to Ouarzazate in the High Atlas, passing through the Valley of Roses and the Valley of a Thousand Kasbahs, built among palm trees.

They arrived in this city, famous for being the gateway to the Sahara, from their citadel in Taurirt. Home to a 19th-century palace, the beautiful landscape, known as the Hollywood of Africa, had served as a backdrop for film shoots.

They loved getting to know the places of their ancestors, who belonged to the Alaoui dynasty.

Rania's cell phone rang. It was her father, giving her the news and asking her not to rush back, to take their time because something unexpected had happened. Hassna's uncle, Manssur, after transferring his house to Idir, a gambling debtor, had retired to his cell and was found dead shortly afterwards. He had hanged himself from the bars, forming a rope knotted with pieces of his clothing.

Rania broke the news to Hassna, but despite everything, she felt compassion for her father's only brother, who had long since lost his mind.

That afternoon, the hitman had received a call from the detective before he delivered the coup de grâce to Hassna. He had asked him to stop the job, saying that it would be pointless to kill the girl, since Manssur was in prison and had finally committed suicide, and no one would pay them for the job.

Once her uncle died and she was convinced that her life was no longer in danger, the girls continued their journey. Hassna had suffered greatly and had been hardened by so much pain. Now she only thought about herself and tried to be happy. She found herself alone without a family. She had Rania, her best and only friend, and that was enough for her.

They entered the ancient imperial city, the economic center of western Morocco, Marrakech. They saw a medieval-style walled city dating back to the Berber Empire. They entered via Bab Jdid Avenue and arrived at the Palace Hotel, adorned with beautiful gardens and palm groves. Inside, they saw magnificent, spacious rooms with carved arches, fine tapestries, beautiful carpets, and walls decorated with Moorish-style tiles. They booked a double room and went down to dinner on the terrace by the pool. As they walked, they saw an interior terrace with a large pool surrounded by Moorish-style arches covered with tiles and carvings. They sat down and ordered a meat kefta tagine, shared the large dish, and drank orange juice. Such freedom seemed incredible; they felt independent, without having to explain themselves to anyone, masters of their own destiny.

After dinner, they retired to their beautifully decorated room with a large terrace overlooking the pool. Hassna, tired from driving even though she took turns with Rania, decided to treat herself to a massage, accompanied by relaxing music, a candlelit dinner, and the delicious aromas of the hotel spa. , they entered the beautiful jacuzzi located in the middle of a large room, surrounded by columns adorned with Moorish-style tiles. They drank fresh orange juice, took the opportunity to do their hair and nails, and once ready, they returned to their room to change and go to the hotel lounge where a band was playing.

The musicians wore long white tunics down to their ankles (Suriyah) and a typical brown and maroon African cap (Kufi) on their heads. They played instruments such as the drum, the darbuka, the bendir (a frame drum similar to a tambourine), the oud (an Arabic guitar), and the flute, performing Gnawa music.

"It's a wonderful place to spend your vacation," Rania said cheerfully. "This is Dad's favorite hotel, but I hadn't realized it was so luxurious."

"That's true," added Hassna, "it's a palace."

That night, after enjoying the Gnawa music, they retired to their room, exhausted from the long journey but happy to have arrived in Marrakech, the red city.

The next day, they woke up late and opened their eyes to the intense midday brightness. The light pierced through the windows like daggers, and when they drew the curtains, the clear, blinding light flooded the room. The day promised to be clear, dressed in a resplendent blue. They ordered breakfast in their room. The day was so sunny that the sky reflected a deep blue in the pool water.

Hassna remembered reminding Hamid that she had once mentioned visiting Marrakech, but she quickly dismissed the idea and stopped thinking about it. They went to have breakfast on the terrace of their room overlooking the pool and surrounding gardens. They asked the waiter what places they could visit nearby, and he told them that they could find brochures on the best places to visit next to the administration office on the first floor. However, he recommended that they not miss the Bahia Palace and the Agdal Gardens, whose 400 hectares feature groves of orange, lemon, and fig trees, as well as countless fruit trees. They hired a taxi from the hotel and decided to visit the Bahia Palace.

The large rectangular courtyards, surrounded by columns forming arches, contrasted green with orange ornamentation, giving it a majestic appearance with its Moorish architectural style. Inside, the luxury was impressive; the ceilings were a work of art in painting and carving with Arabic designs. The entrance doors were surrounded by blue, white, and ochre tiles. The doors were almost entirely carved and led to beautiful gardens and fountains everywhere, with different designs. The floors of the terraces where the water fountains were located were hexagonal in shape and covered with greenish-ochre tiles, predominantly blue, a Moroccan color, and white, symbolizing purity.

The harem courtyard caught her attention, where the prime minister had four wives and twenty-four concubines.

"Can you imagine, Hassna, sharing your man with other wives?"

"I can't imagine it, Rania, because my condition for marrying will be to be the only wife."

"I think the same; we are in a different era."

They left the Bahia Palace and went to pray at the Koutoubia Mosque, a beautiful reddish mosque seventy meters high located in the medina of Jamaa El-Fenna. They entered the impressive square tower, surrounded by palm groves. In front of it was a large fountain in high relief, forming three large round tiled floors. They walked a long way between a rectangular fountain and black iron benches on either side, until they entered barefoot through a large white carved arch with six marble columns. Inside, there was a series of white columns forming rows of arches over red ochre carpets with rectangular designs typical of Arab carpets. The ceiling lamps hung in the shape of bells, with decorations hanging like crystal and bronze stalactites.

After thanking Allah for bringing them back safely, the taxi took them back to the hotel after leaving the mosque. On the way, they hired the taxi driver again to take them to dinner at 8:00 p.m. at a Moroccan restaurant that offered Arabic dance shows, and to pick them up at the same place at midnight. The taxi driver agreed to take them.

They arrived at the hotel to rest in their room and get ready for the evening.

The taxi driver arrived punctually at the hotel to pick them up. They already had the perfect place to have dinner and see the belly dancing show. They headed to Echouhada Avenue, a place that had been recommended to them and where they had booked a table in advance. When they arrived, the place was packed with people eating and waiting for the reserved tables to become available. At one of the tables, Hassna thought she saw Hamid and her heart skipped a beat. A fleeting flash ran through her chest, but when the figure turned around, she realized it had been a mirage of her imagination and sadly continued on her way. They descended a large staircase and arrived at a spacious reception area surrounded by dining rooms on both sides. The room was dimly lit by lamps hanging from the ceiling, giving it an enigmatic and romantic air.

The restaurant was decorated in exquisite Moroccan style, with beautiful, comfortable cushions on the chairs at the tables for to sit and savor the delicious dishes. Each table had candles that lit up the room. As their reservation was delayed by thirty minutes, they were taken to the waiting room: a beautiful enclosed garden with very comfortable seating and a small table in the center adorned with green tropical plants cascading down the walls and black lanterns with candlelight and soft music that gave off a romantic aura.

They came to serve them and gave them the drinks menu to order from. They only had fresh orange juice and some appetizers that were brought in a tagine, a typical Moroccan pot. They drank and chatted while their table was being prepared.

It was the first time they had been alone in a restaurant with a belly dancing show. Everything they saw seemed incredible to them. They found it fascinating to have so much freedom and, above all, not to have to worry about their financial situation, as they both had plenty of money and no one demanded schedules or anything like that from them. Hassna was alone in the world, without a family, and Rania, since her parents divorced, had been living in a boarding school. When her father left, he gave her a house and a car so she could live with Aurora, a young woman who was her secretary's sister. Aurora had been with Rania for a long time and had also been her guardian, as well as being in charge of approving her outings and spending the money Rania received from her father. Now she could take on that responsibility with her recent emancipation upon turning fifteen.

They both lived in a wonderful world and did whatever they wanted.

Their table was ready, so they went over and sat down. They ordered soft drinks and a lamb tagine seasoned with almonds, dates, and lemon, eggplant with couscous, and for dessert, peanut cake with strawberries, Arabic sponge cake with honey, and the usual mint tea.

They both enjoyed the dinner and the atmosphere.

"What time is the ballroom dancing show?" Hassna asked excitedly.

"Maybe after or during dinner," replied Rania.

Suddenly, the lights went out and the only light left was from the candles on the tables and the lanterns.

The music began and the dancers appeared one by one between the tables. They were beautiful women wearing exotic two-piece outfits in different colors, with skirts and bras decorated with rhinestones, silk, and medals. They wore gold bracelets on their hands and ankles and veils on their heads. They swayed their hips, shoulders, arms, and hands in a smooth and sensual manner.

One of the dancers entered with a large bronze tray full of lit candles on her head, dancing and maintaining her balance, while another held a saber above her head, dancing next to each table. After the show, the dancers invited the audience to dance.

Rania and Hassna danced, giving an excellent performance and receiving applause. They returned to their seats happy and satisfied with this enchanting evening. They were discovering the world in a fast and intense way.

After dinner, the taxi was waiting to take them back to the hotel. They arrived at midnight happy, with no one scolding them for being late, and stayed up chatting until two in the morning, when they fell asleep, waking up at noon.

The morning breeze caressed their window as they stretched and ordered breakfast in their room, almost at lunchtime. They leafed through some excursion catalogs and thought about traveling to the Atlantic coast: Essaouira, formerly Mogador, a place Hamid had told Hassna he would like to take her someday.

They enjoyed that afternoon in Marrakech, visiting the Koranic studies center, which housed beautiful examples of Moroccan art and architecture. They continued through the interior of the elongated medina, where the bodies of those executed were once displayed. They walked through the streets, shops, corners, and alleys, among the stores selling veils, jewelry, and shoes. They left the medina as the sun began to rise over the city. The days passed without them realizing it or even knowing what they were saying.

At Hassna's request, in memory of Hamid, she was excited about the idea of exploring Essaouira, formerly Mogador, six hours and eighteen minutes away on the Atlantic coast of Morocco. They set off on their journey full of excitement, without rushing, enjoying the sunny day with a map in hand, and embarking on another adventure with joy and freedom. During the trip, they stopped to eat something and stretch their legs. They went into a small restaurant and ordered briouat, a tasty triangular pastry filled with meat, cheese, lemon, and pepper. They bought two more sweet pastries for the road and bottles of coconut water, which they had run out of.

On the way, Rania looked at Hassna and asked her what she planned to do when she returned: live in Granada or Malaga.

Hassna replied that she would like to return to her parents' house and enroll at the University of Malaga to study business administration.

She encouraged Rania to move in with her so they could attend the same university. Rania thought about it for a while; the idea seemed like a nice change of scenery.

Her father had an apartment facing the sea in Malaga, and she could borrow it to live there. Hassna insisted that she stay with her in her house, which was large and located in the best neighborhood in Malaga.

After lunch, they continued their journey. They were in no hurry and could enjoy themselves to the fullest.

On the way to Essaouira, they passed through vast argan forests where the trees winked at the herd of goats and the horizon was dotted with hundreds of trees under a bright and comforting sun. They stopped along the way and entered a cooperative where they were shown how the oil was made. They bought several bottles of oil, creams, and scented soaps.

"Hamid told me that this city was once an ancient Portuguese citadel and that its walls hide many picturesque corners steeped in history. Let's continue our journey; we're almost there, we're two hours and thirty-five minutes from our destination," Hassna said cheerfully.

They entered the medina of Essaouira, protected by walls facing the coast. The gentle breeze rustled the trees and accompanied the soft whisper of the leaves. They entered the central square, Moulay Hassan, at the entrance to Bab Marrakech, where artisans sold their wood and fabric products. They left and headed to the souk, to a jewelry store, and bought more gold necklaces to wear on their hands and feet, as well as hijabs in different colors. While choosing them, Hassna said to Rania:

"To think that not long ago I used to hide as I walked, lowering my covered head, looking at the ground to go unnoticed, covering my face with the hijab when I wasn't wearing the burqa. Those were the days, dear Rania! You have no idea how scared I was to travel. I felt completely alone and abandoned, lost, scared, in a strange place surrounded by strangers facing unexpected incidents, some much worse than others. I don't know how I didn't go completely crazy.

"What a shame, my friend," Rania replied. "And on top of that, no cell phone coverage, which had me very worried because I didn't hear from you."

"I didn't hear from you either, and with the detective following me like a shadow everywhere I went... But now I'm free, it's all over, and I'm starting a new life."

Hassna remembered Hamid. "What will become of him? Will he remember me?" she thought. "I don't want to get my hopes up, ever again. I don't want to suffer for love or anything else. I'm going to devote myself to studying and having fun."

"There are lots of activities in this place to enjoy and have fun, Rania." It looks like a bright desert facing the sea, where we can ride along the shore on horseback or dromedaries, or hike along the Atlantic coast to the dunes and sunbathe. What do you think?

"Okay, my friend! Let's enjoy the trip and forget our worries and problems!" added Rania enthusiastically.

They checked into a luxurious hotel overlooking the bay. Their room faced the sea, where the waves broke mercilessly against the shore and frightened the little seagulls flying fearfully over the sand. They rested in that beautiful place and spent the night until the next day.

The first rays of dawn appeared on the horizon, the sky was clear, and the sea was calm. A cool breeze lit up the day under a fiery blue sky.

They stretched and took advantage of the day to get ready and go horseback riding, since they had spent most of their time riding dromedaries in the desert. They rode at high speed to feel the wind on their faces and mitigate the heat of the sun, and watched people enjoying water sports, surfing, and jet skis.

"Can you imagine Rania us riding motorcycles or jet skis without hijabs and in swimsuits?" Hassna announced as she watched the boys doing stunts on the sea.

"Not really, my friend. Our culture is very oriented toward laws and rules, control and regulations. We can't wear pants or show our arms or hair."

"But no one knows us here, and no one sees us."

"What about Allah?" Rania asked, staring at Hassna.

"That's right, my friend. Let's go to the fishing port. I really feel like eating seafood and fish. This place is famous for its food; well, that's what Dad says," Hassna said.

They headed for the fishing port, where a large colony of nesting seagulls watched the visitors with curiosity. They found numerous shops, artisans, and artists offering their wares at reasonable prices. They entered a typical Moroccan market restaurant, where the menu was written in white chalk on a blackboard.

"Let's order mint tea, a seafood tagine to share, two fresh orange juices, and fruit with honey for dessert. Sounds good to me, I love it."

After eating, they relaxed by strolling through the market. They untied their horses and galloped toward the beach where they had rented them, shouting "freedom!" as they made their way. The beach was sandy and long, with palm trees reaching the shore and a r bathed by gentle waves under the cobalt blue sky that would soon begin to redden in the west. The girls stopped riding and dismounted happily, heading to a modest fruit stand for fresh orange juice to quench their thirst on a hot day.

They walked back to the hotel overlooking the sea. Inside, they admired the exquisite Moroccan decor, with arches, columns, and staircases adorned with Moorish tiles, beautiful artwork, a spa, and unique gardens.

They arrived at their bedroom, removed their hijabs and tunics, and refreshed themselves with a bath before heading to the spa, where they received a relaxing massage with deliciously scented oils and aromatic ointments.

They thought they would spend three wonderful days in this enigmatic place, but it was time to return to Spain after several months away. They appreciated one last time the brilliant hue of the sea, with the spectacular sunset they enjoyed from the terrace of their room, listening to the plaintive cries of the seagulls flying overhead and breaking the calm of the afternoon, as the sun descended from the sky and the sea sparkled like a diamond mine. The moment of calm that preceded the sunset was over, and a gentle breeze blew, immersed in twilight meditation, and the pale light of a shy moon hovered over an endless beach of fine golden sand. And night fell.

The next morning, the first light of dawn surprised Rania. An intense halo of light emanated from inside the room, waking Hassna with the metallic sound of her haughty voice: "Wake up, we're late." Hassna hurried out, stealthy as a cat under the sheets. The city was waking up in unison and the light of dawn was shining brightly, giving the day a touch of joy and hope.

They checked out and the hotel taxi took them to Mogador airport, from where they flew to Tangier. From there, they took the flight to Granada.

Granada

They landed at Federico García Lorca Airport in Granada.

"Finally home!" said Rania.

Hassna smiled and replied,

"Yes, now we have nothing to fear; we are free as the wind."

They each picked up their carry-on luggage and entered customs, showing their passports. They looked at each other with a smile and a knowing glance. They took a taxi and headed to Rania's apartment.

Rania's father had informed her that, following Manssur's suicide, his house had passed into the hands of the debtor Idir and that, following his orders, the maid had removed Hassna's belongings and stored them in a safe place, along with her aunt Lalla's jewelry. He told her that when she arrived, he would take them to Rania's apartment.

They made themselves comfortable and Hassna made two phone calls: one to Amal, Lalla's loyal employee, asking her to go to Rania's apartment and drop off her things, promising to pay for transportation.

The other call was to her former nanny, Jamila, her employee in Malaga, asking her to go to the house and wait for her, as she was coming back to stay for good and would arrive over the weekend.

Hassna tried to convince Rania to go with her to Malaga, but Rania had many things to resolve before leaving with her.

"When I'm done with all my preparations, I'll go, I promise."

Hassna accepted the deal and after spending a few days with her friend and packing her bags with the things Amal had brought her, they said goodbye with the promise to see each other soon.

Malaga

Upon arriving in Malaga, Hassna left the Costa del Sol airport and headed to catch a taxi to go home. As she entered the city, she felt nostalgic for her childhood and reconnected with the breeze, the sun, and the streets of the city of her childhood. Episodes from her life with her parents and Omar came to mind. She also remembered moments of great pain, such as the loss of her parents, the move to Granada to live with her unknown aunt and uncle, and Omar's death. She shed a few tears, but soon found the strength to enjoy the journey, leaving the bitter taste behind.

She arrived home and her nanny Jamila was waiting for her with love and tenderness.

"My little girl! How wonderful to see you looking so beautiful and grown up!" They hugged each other affectionately.

"Come on, come inside, I'll take your luggage to your room."

"Thank you, Nana, back home and this time forever."

"Praise be to Allah, my daughter."

Jamila surprised her with mint tea with dates and almond sweets.

"Shukran."

"I've prepared the food my daughter loves so much. I hope you enjoy it," said Jamila affectionately.

"Shukran, Nana," said Hassna as she approached and gave Jamila a warm kiss.

"Your nanny is old, but my little girl will be treated like a princess."

Hassna smiled and accepted the date tea as she told Jamila about her escape and dangerous adventure in the desert. The nanny said,

"My child! How sad! Thank Allah that he brought you back safe and sound. What are your plans, child?" asked Jamila.

"I've been thinking, Nana. First, I'll go see Fahim to see how things are going at the Madrid office. Rania's father took care of transferring my inheritance. Now I want Fahim, as my father's and now my partner, to advise me on everything that concerns me. Then I'm thinking of going to college to study business administration so I don't fall behind. Nana, we need a car. The one in the garage probably doesn't work. The battery must be dead, and it's old. I'll take care of transportation tomorrow."

"How you've grown, my girl! It seems like yesterday when I was getting your clothes ready to take you to school. You've become a young woman and you're very pretty."

"Shukran nana, I'm sixteen now. Time has flown by with so many unexpected events that I forgot my birthday. I'm starting a new phase in my life and I'll turn to Fahim for guidance on everything related to my father's business . They are now the closest thing I have to a family."

"Very well thought out, my daughter, they were great friends of your parents."

The next day, Hassna contacted Fahim, who treated her with great kindness.

"I'm glad to hear from you, dear Hassna. I know from your lawyer that you have been granted your parents' inheritance."

"That's why I'm calling you, Fahim. I'd like to know if we can meet and ask your advice."

"Of course, Hassna, whatever you want. Latifa also wants to see you. Can you come tomorrow? We can talk more calmly here. We'll wait for you at lunchtime."

"I'll be there tomorrow, thank you."

Hassna went to the dealership and bought a white convertible sports car from the same year, paying for it with a check from one of her companies.

Thrilled with the purchase of her first car, she went home to show it to her nanny.

She entered the house and called Jamila:

"Jamila! I bought a car, let's go try it out."

"My dear, it's very nice, but it doesn't have a roof... Our veils will fly away. We'll have to hold them tight. Where shall we go?"

"First, to the supermarket to fill up the empty pantry," said Hassna excitedly.

"But, my dear, the groceries won't fit in this car."

"That's true, Nana, I know, we'll do the shopping and send it by taxi."

Jamila smiled and shook her head.

"All right, my child."

The next day, Hassna woke up very excited to go to Fahim and Latifa's house. She chose a pretty dress that matched her scarf, ate breakfast, and called Rania on the phone.

"Rania, you have to come see my beautiful car. I bought it yesterday and I'm very happy. I'm going to Fahim and Latifa's house at noon. They've invited me to lunch and then we'll talk business."

"I'm glad, Hassna, I'm very happy for you."

"Me too, my friend, and I'll be even happier the day you come to Malaga."

I'm in that situation, I'll have to talk to my father because I want to move.

"Talk to him immediately."

"I will, Hassna, goodbye."

Hassna, under the bright sky that quickened her pace, set off on her journey and arrived punctually at Fahim's house, where Latifa welcomed her.

"Salam aleikum, Hassna."

"Wa alaikum assalam," Hassna replied.

"Come in, make yourself comfortable. You look very pretty."

"Shukran bezaf; thank you very much," Hassna replied.

Latifa then brought mint tea and almond sweets.

Fahim came in and gave Hassna a warm hug.

"Welcome home, Hassna; sit down and enjoy some tea before we go to the dining room. So you've moved to Malaga?"

"That's right, Fahim. Since Uncle Manssur and Lalla passed away, I have nothing to do in Granada. You know that their house went to a creditor, so I thought I'd come home."

"Very wise, Hassna; you know we love you like a daughter. Your parents and I were very good friends, and we've known you since you were little."

There was a nostalgic silence during which they remembered their beloved Omar, and then they continued their conversation.

"I'll bring you up to date on company matters, which will help you stay abreast of what other companies are doing. In a month, we'll travel to Madrid, to the head office. There's a board meeting, and as the majority shareholder, you'll be introduced at the meeting, so we have time to brief you on how the company operates. We have qualified staff and the company has been running smoothly in recent years, but I understand that you have every right to be present at company events. So we have four weeks to bring you up to speed on everything. This afternoon, after lunch, we'll start in my office. Hassna smiled and accepted the offer of help."

"Look, Fahim, I'll do my best to learn. I've just started studying business administration at university."

"Yes, Hassna, but practice is perhaps more important, you'll see."

"Shukran Fahim, I knew I could count on you."

"That's right, Hassna, we're like family."

Hassna returned home very excited. From the little Fahim had explained to her that afternoon, she was sure she would learn diligently and soon be ready to present herself to the board.

Morocco

Hamid's father fell ill and was taken to a hospital in Marrakesh. Due to concerns about the current situation of the business "Las Jaimas de Lujo," he suffered a pre-heart attack, which shocked his children living in Madrid. They had to travel urgently to Marrakesh.

"Why does Dad need to work?" Hassan asked indignantly. "We have to make him see reason. He was lucky this time, but if he continues to insist on working, he'll end up dead."

"We all understand, Hassan, but how do we do it?"

144

"Maybe we could suggest that he sell Las Jaimas de Lujo and get rid of the hotel, leaving him only with the breeding and sale of horses. But I can already hear him, brother; he'll say that they'll give him a pittance for the business because of the lack of tourists."

"I have an idea," said Hamid. "What if we tell him that someone is interested in buying it?"

"And who would that be?"

"Us, but under another name." Hamid looked hopeful.

"I'd say he won't sell it."

"But if we ask him how much he would sell it for, maybe we could buy it together and let Rasta Boy manage it?"

"Would he be willing?"

"He's been working with my father for years, he's his right-hand man. If it doesn't work out, we'll sell it."

"We should take him to Madrid to recover."

"Okay, but who's going to take the plunge? My father is stubborn, and when I bring it up, he goes round and round in circles and nothing gets done."

Three weeks passed and Habbib recovered. His children asked him to travel with them to Madrid for a month before returning to the desert. After several hours of insistence, he agreed to accompany them, but only for a couple of weeks.

Malaga, one month later.

Early Monday morning, Hassna waited for Fahim at the airport to fly to Madrid, to the head office. Hassna was a little nervous and excited as she was to be introduced as the majority shareholder of

145

the company. She arrived at the airport looking like a spring flower, driving her white convertible, dressed in an elegant and sober navy blue skirt suit and a blue veil with white polka dots to match her outfit. Fahim greeted her and told her she looked very beautiful and professional.

Madrid

They entered the building, headed for the elevator, and arrived at the top floor. On the way, the elevator stopped on the eighth floor, the " " floor. Hassna was busy with her briefcase when she heard a familiar voice addressing Fahim.

"Salam aleikum."

"Alaikum assalam, Hamid."

Hassna stopped looking at her briefcase and was surprised to see Hamid in front of her, a ray of light shining in his dark eyes. The daggers of light were silhouetted between the half-open elevator doors.

"What a pleasant surprise!" exclaimed Hamid. "I haven't heard from you in a long time, Hassna. What are you doing here?"

"Do you two know each other?" Fahim asked in surprise.

"Of course. If it weren't for Hamid, I wouldn't be here. He saved my life twice in Morocco."

"Is that true?" asked Fahim, surprised.

"That's right, man," replied Hamid.

"And you, Fahim? How do you know each other?" asked Hassna.

"He's Latifa's nephew. What a small world!

"And what do you do in this building?" asked Hassna.

"I work here in the legal department with my brother Hassan, in our offices on the 8th and 9th floors. What about you, Hassna?"

"I'm here to ask Fahim to introduce me to the board of directors as a majority shareholder."

"Congratulations, I'm glad to hear it. Let's see if we can meet up."

"I'm afraid my visit will be brief. We'll be back in Malaga when the meeting is over." Hassna felt her heart pounding and her hands were drenched in sweat, which bothered her.

Hamid gave her his business card with his phone number so they could stay in touch, while admiring Hassna's stunning beauty and the boundless energy she exuded, wrapped in that beautiful woman's body.

"Shukran bezaf Hamid, I don't have any cards right now, but I can give you my other phone number in Malaga."

"It's been a pleasure to meet you, Hassna; you're very beautiful."

"Shukran bezaf, Hamid."

Hamid said goodbye to his uncle and stayed on the ninth floor.

At that moment, Fahim said to Hassna:

"You'll have to tell me how my nephew saved your life twice."

The elevator stopped on the top floor and they headed to the office. She tried to hide from Fahim how nervous she felt about the unexpected encounter.

Hamid was impressed to see Hassna looking so beautiful, dressed in western style and wearing a Moroccan veil. He spent the whole morning thinking about her. "I have to see her again, even if I have to travel to Malaga. It's a shame she's leaving so soon; otherwise, I would have invited her to lunch."

Hassna entered the office with a haughty and serene look, showing her beautiful eyes, eager and warmly captivating, with her sharp nose looking straight ahead, more beautiful than the sun. Her uncle was prouder than a peacock wearing a tie.

Hassna for her part, had Hamid on her mind and had to make an effort to attend the meeting and not make a fool of herself. Fahim introduced Hassna Sabal Saadi, the daughter of the former owner, the magnate Assim Sabal, now heir to the company and largest shareholder. Everyone was captivated by the young executive.

After the meeting, Fahim congratulated her on her manners, her elegant and dignified discussion, and her splendid maturity in leading the meeting. Her feminine charm and the fluid precision of her words earned her the admiration of those attending the shareholders' meeting.

Before leaving for the airport, Fahim announced:

"We'll have lunch at the restaurant across from the building. Most of the executives from nearby offices go there, and they serve international cuisine."

Hassna accepted the invitation.

When they sat down at the table for lunch, Hamid came in, approached his uncle's table, and asked to join them for lunch.

"Sit down nephew," Fahim replied. "We meet again."

"How did the meeting go, Hassna?" Hamid asked.

"Pretty well, I think," Hassna replied.

"I think so too, very well," emphasized Fahim, quite the executive, and winked at Hamid. "I'm advising her on her business. I'm sure she'll do wonderfully."

"You're going to make me blush, Fahim," added Hassna. During lunch, Hassna displayed a soft, melodious laugh and fluid, refined conversation, with a sense of elegance and premature maturity.

That night, back in Malaga, she told Fahim all about her trip to Morocco and her experience in the desert during the flight.

"He's a golden boy, very hardworking, and always leaves a mark of honesty in his work, just like his family. He's single. He would be good for you, Hassna. He would make a good husband."

Hassna remained silent, professing sacramental respect for her uncle, and changed the subject.

Hassna thought.

"No wonder he reminded me of Omar, he was his first cousin he never talked about him, maybe because he lived in the desert."

Malaga

Upon arriving in Malaga, Hassna said goodbye to Fahim until the next day, when she would return home.

Back home, Fahim told Latifa about his encounter with his nephew Hamid and the surprising encounter he had with Hassna during his trip to the desert. Latifa was very happy that her late sister's son was friends with Hassna.

"That boy is ideal to be Hassna's husband," Latifa commented.

"That's true woman, but times have changed. Girls choose their partners now, although I saw them as very good friends," replied Fahim.

"I'll encourage him to come visit us, maybe the kids will fall in love," Latifa said. Fahim smiled.

Back home, Hassna barely slept that night, so excited was she about the trip, the introduction at the gathering, and finally, the two meetings with Hamid, Omar's cousin. It was enough for one day.

That night she had a beautiful romantic dream about Hamid; they were in the desert and on a moonlit night, he stretched a silver bridge over the sand. They kissed and Hamid carried her in his arms to his tent. The sky was studded with stars stretching across the horizon, while the moonlight smiled through the clearings. He laid her down on colorful cushions as the steam of his burning heat enveloped her like a fiery mist, then they explored each other's bodies, feeling their kisses and caresses until he made her his, feeling it deep within her being, she enjoying it to the fullest until she reached climax and touched the sky. When she woke up, she found herself upset, sweaty, and wet between her legs.

"But what is this? What is happening to me and Hamid? I know for sure, I'm going crazy! I'm not going to fall in love, I don't want to fall in love! and that's that," Hassna thought fervently.

She showered, got dressed, and went out to the dining room, where Jamila had prepared breakfast for her with freshly baked rolls, cheese, honey, and fresh orange juice.

"Shukran Nana, but I don't have much of an appetite."

"You have to eat, girl, otherwise how are you going to do well in your studies?" She approached her, her round face covered by a veil, and said, "I'll go with you."

After breakfast, Hassna went to the University of Malaga (UMA) to find out about admission and other details. She gathered information and then went to Fahim's house.

Latifa welcomed her warmly.

"Come in, Hassna, Fahim is waiting for you in his office."

"Shukran, Latifa."

Long, languid, and fruitful months passed, and Hassna learned more every day from Fahim and also at university, where she earned excellent grades.

"You are very intelligent, Hassna. You will soon become an excellent executive. Your father, Assim, may he rest in peace with Allah, will be very proud of you. You have made great progress."

"Shukran, Fahim, I owe it all to you."

Madrid

Hamid and Hassan managed to convince their father to sell "Las Jaimas de Lujo" to a supposed hotel company.

"You can go back to the desert, but you'll only see the livestock; you won't have to worry about whether there are tourists or not. The sale is done and the money is in your account. From now on, you'll have to fend for yourself if we can't get you back to Madrid." Habbib remained silent and very obedient, thinking that he would soon return to the desert.

Malaga

Hassna interrupted her studies and called Rania to see what she had decided.

"I'm sorry, my friend, I still won't be able to move to Malaga. My father has advised me to finish the first two semesters at the University of Granada and then move to Malaga. I think he wants to see me more often now. But I'll be able to visit you during the holidays."

"What a shame, Rania, I was really looking forward to seeing you again."

"Me too."

Hassna was saddened by Rania's response and thought that time would pass quickly and that she would wait for the holidays to see her, even though they saw each other every night on their cell phones and talked for a long time.

Fahim thought about inviting Hamid and Hassna to lunch so they could get to know each other better. Hamid accepted his uncle Fahim's invitation.

"Nephew, the office jet will be waiting for you at the usual hangar to take you to Malaga. I would love to see my brother-in-law. I know he is convalescing in Madrid. Perhaps he would like to make the trip."

"Thank you, Uncle Fahim, but my father has already returned to Morocco with my brother."

"What a pity, I would have loved to see him."

"Now that he doesn't have so much work, I'll let him know every time I come to take him to Malaga to visit you. I'll be with you this weekend," Hamid replied cheerfully.

"We'll be delighted to wait for you, nephew," added Fahim.

Fahim didn't tell Hassna that Hamid was invited that weekend, so that the meeting would be informal, with nothing planned.

Early Friday morning, Hamid headed to the airport and took the flight to Malaga. He was elegantly dressed in casual attire: a long-sleeved white cotton shirt and light-colored pants that matched his loafers.

Fahim's car was waiting for him when he arrived. It was a sunny morning and the trees sparkled in the sunlight.

He stepped off the company jet, put on his sunglasses, and looked like a magazine model, with his sleeves rolled up and two buttons of his shirt undone, exposing part of his chest and revealing a virile air. He quickened his pace and uncle and nephew embraced.

"It's so good to see you again, son! We should visit each other more often. Life flies by without you even noticing," Fahim said. They walked arm in arm to the car waiting for them on the tarmac, and after settling into their seats and the driver stowing Hamid's luggage in the trunk, uncle and nephew struck up a conversation.

"Nephew, tell me how you're doing, apart from the law firm."

Hamid smiled.

"My life is very quiet, Uncle. After work, I sometimes go to the movies or the theater. I like to read and I have a few friends. Lately, I've been taking care of my father in the hospital and then at home. Even though we had a nurse with him all the time, we didn't leave him alone. We tried to talk him out of leaving and going to work, but you know how stubborn he is. He wouldn't leave the desert for anything in the world; it's his life."

"That's Hamid for you; when you're older, you don't want to accept that you have to stop working."

It was a beautiful morning, the weather was cool, and the sun was trying to peek through. The streets looked clean and glamorous, and Hamid remembered Hassna, the day he saw her in the elevator on his way to the office.

"I wanted to ask you, Fahim, how do you know Hassna?" Hamid asked, very interested.

"Nephew, I've known Hassna since she was born. She's like our own daughter. Her parents and I were close friends and partners in the Madrid company. I've known Hassna since her mother was carrying her in her womb. Unfortunately, she was orphaned at a very young age due to the plane crash."

"Yes, uncle, she told me everything that happened after her parents' death and that she had to travel to Granada to see her father's brother."

"Son, it was the worst thing that could have happened to that poor girl. So, when he wrote that will, he may not have known about his brother Manssur's vices."

"She also told me that she was about to get married and that her fiancé had died."

"Unfortunately, nephew, those were the worst moments of our lives... Our dear Omar passed away so young."

"But... what does Omar have to do with Hassna?" Hamid asked curiously.

"Didn't she tell you about Omar?"

"Honestly, no, she didn't tell me her fiancé's name. You're not going to tell me who he was..."

"Yes, son, Hassna's fiancé was Omar, my son, your cousin."

Hamid was shocked, almost speechless.

"That would have been the wedding Hassna's parents dreamed of. She's a wonderful girl and they would have been very happy, as I told you. Hassna is like our daughter. I hope she finds a good man who deserves her."

Hamid was surprised at how small the world was.

"Since you live far away, we haven't seen each other much. Your father couldn't come to Omar's funeral. Only your brother and his wife came. It was all very sudden."

"I remember that at the time I was traveling around Morocco on business related to the horse trade, and it was difficult for me to get here," Hamid said solemnly.

Latifa entered the room and greeted Hamid.

"Salam aleikum, Hamid."

"Alaikum assalam, Latifa."

"I'm glad to see you, Hamid, after several years."

"Likewise, auntie."

"You look very handsome, you're quite the man now. I'm glad you accepted our invitation. Your uncle told me about your father's illness. How is my brother-in-law?"

"He's back in Morocco and he's better."

The maid entered the room with a tray of mint tea and coconut, almond, and sesame sweets. She poured three small glasses, pouring the tea from a high position, as is customary and a sign of hospitality.

"Fahim, you were telling me, dear aunt, about the relationship between Hassna's parents and you."

"Indeed, Hamid, we were very good friends and excellent parents, and they will be enjoying Allah's kingdom, just like our Omar."

"As Hamid learned more about Hassna and her family, his admiration and respect for her grew. He admired her strength, her determination to succeed, her simplicity adorned with delicacy, her clear gaze that allowed him to guess her thoughts. She was dynamic and quiet, with a wise sweetness despite her young age. She had had to mature, and that made her strong in her decisions.

At that moment, the employee was heard to say:

"Salam Aleikum, Miss Hassna."

"Alaikum assalam," Hassna replied with a big smile.

"Come into the living room, miss, they're waiting for you."

Hassna entered elegantly dressed, her hair covered by a veil that matched her dress. She greeted everyone and was surprised to see that Hamid had also been invited; they both looked gorgeous. When she saw him, she blushed and everyone noticed. Hassna felt her face and ears burning, which made her feel uncomfortable.

She sat down and pretended to eat a sesame sweet and drink a small glass of mint tea. The color slowly drained from her face. Hamid couldn't take his eyes off her; without looking at him, she could feel the force of his gaze, with those eyes sunk beneath his bushy eyebrows.

Hamid seized the opportunity and said to her:

"I know from Fahim that he is advising you on the development of the business and that you are very dedicated."

"Yes," Hassna replied timidly. "I come every day, he explains things to me in a simple way, and I'm learning."

156

"It can't be easy for such a young girl to supervise so many companies."

She replied with a smile: "I've also started college and am studying business administration, and with Fahim's advice, everything seems easier. He's a very good teacher," said Hassna, smiling again.

Hamid was captivated by that beautiful smile, which revealed the white pearls of her mouth, and a voice as soft as cotton.

They then moved on to lunch and enjoyed delicious Moroccan dishes, eating with their right hands, sitting on luxurious colorful cushions. Spread out on the table were various dishes, including lamb stews, couscous, vegetables, olives, and delicious desserts, which they shared.

After lunch, the men left the table to smoke shisha hookah, or water pipe with different flavored tobacco.

Latifa played Moroccan music and Fahim asked the women to dance for them. At first, Hassna was reluctant, but Latifa began to dance and Hassna joined in.

Both gave a beautiful performance. Hassna covered herself with a large veil or malea made of thick black fabric, which she rolled up and unrolled, slowly revealing her body and showing freedom, sensuality, harmony, and delicacy in her dance.

Those present celebrated the performance. Hamid saw her dance for the second time. The previous time, he had spied on her without her noticing in the desert, dressed in her two-piece costume with medals and sequins adorning her beautiful legs, which he had etched into his mind.

They spent a lovely evening together. Hamid invited Hassna out the next day, as he needed to take advantage of the weekend to be with her. Hassna gladly accepted the invitation.

The next morning, Hamid arrived in one of his uncle's cars and showed up at Hassna's house with the intention of going for a walk and taking advantage of the beautiful sunny day to enjoy themselves together. Hassna was ready and waiting for Hamid, a little nervous as she felt intimidated. Perhaps because he was ten years older than her, she felt inexperienced next to him.

When Hamid came down to pick her up, he surprised her with a bouquet of red roses and was impressed by how beautiful she looked. They greeted each other and she nervously thanked him for the gesture.

Hamid had planned to take her to Antequera, to the Rock of Lovers, a place he had not yet had the opportunity to visit. Hassna asked him where they were going, and he asked her if she knew Antequera. She replied that she had been there with her parents when she was little, but that she hardly remembered it.

"I've been told," said Hamid, "that this enclave has the face of a reclining woman. It's a large limestone rock. A legend similar to Romeo and Juliet arose there: two lovers of different religions who, in order to stay together, held hands and jumped into the void."

"I didn't know that story," she replied, blushing.

They walked a few miles and arrived at the place where they could see the mountain with the woman's face looking up at the sky. At its feet, they could see a series of small houses, one next to the other, among green meadows and grazing goats. The sky was clear and intensely blue, the pure air caressed her face, and the golden palm trees shone with the first rays of the sun. The mischievous hand of a hawk took her by surprise and they both fell agonizingly into the abyss of great love, their words burning with every word of

158

love. Reciprocated love gave her the security and strength she had longed for, and her life was filled with a thousand love songs, taking small steps of dawns of repressed anxiety with a heart gone mad.

"Do you like this place?" Hamid asked.

"Yes, very much. It's very peaceful," replied Hassna.

"Like in the desert?"

"Not quite," she replied, smiling nervously.

"You know, Hassna," Hamid said as they walked hand in hand, "I always remember the days in the desert when we walked under the moonlight and the starry sky. From the first time I saw you and rescued you that morning under the scorching sun, I felt a special attraction to you, and since then, I haven't been able to get you out of my mind."

Hassna felt the sweat on her hands and her chest pounding with every word Hamid uttered. Her ears and cheeks were red-hot from how red they were. How many times had she dreamed of this moment, and now all she wanted to do was run away. They were still holding hands, she felt a hard hand and long fingers and bubbles in her chest, the fluttering of a thousand butterflies in her stomach, and she thought she would faint if she continued to hold his hand. He stopped, looked at her with a tender gaze of love and said:

"Hassna, will you marry me?"

He felt an unfathomable abyss of tenderness towards her.

Hassna felt her legs tremble and did not know how to respond. She remained silent, and the red color of her face turned pale. Hamid's words shone in the darkness of her soul. He realized how nervous she was and confirmed it.

"You don't have to answer me now, think about it and let me know what you've decided. From now on, I'll tell you that if we get to something, I'll respect your studies, your activities. I like you because you're strong, intelligent, a fighter, and also a beautiful woman."

The pale color of her face turned red. She was still holding his hand; he had a special attraction for making her feel loved and protected.

Then they drove up a road and gazed at the whole panorama from above, inhaling the warm, fragrant atmosphere. Hassna contemplated the beautiful landscape, but her mind was on Hamid's proposal. She was deeply in love with him, she dreamed of him, she loved him, but she was afraid of love. She would not allow her heart to be broken a second time, but she did not want to lose him either. She felt a series of worries and indecisions take hold of her.

"Happiness has returned to me," she thought sadly. "Shouldn't I take advantage of it to escape from him? I will not close my heart again, as I did before, because that prevented me from loving."

On their way back, they entered an elegant luxury restaurant and enjoyed a fusion of Middle Eastern, Moroccan, and Arabic cuisine.

Hamid never let go of her hand. Hassna felt it almost numb, but she didn't pull away. It gave her pleasure to touch that big, strong, rough hand. After a delicious lunch, they headed home, enjoying a beautiful sunset and agreeing to go out again the next day, as Hassna would give Hamid her answer. He said goodbye to her very formally, and she gave him a tender smile.

When Hassna got home, she went straight to her bedroom, took off her veil and bag, and lay down on the bed to think. Fahim and Latifa had told her that he was a serious, hard-working guy; there was no way he would embarrass her aunt and uncle. Hamid had also

160

told her that he wouldn't interfere with her studies or her decisions; everything was so perfect that it scared her.

She called Rania in Granada to tell her what had happened; she would have to give her an answer the next day. Rania started shouting again.

"Again! You barely know each other! It's true that he's Fahim's nephew and Omar's cousin, but remember that, according to what you've told me, they've lived far away from each other, between Morocco and Madrid. I don't know Hassna, I don't know what to say to you. It all seems very rushed. We're young we do what we want. You're going to marry someone you've only known for a very short time. No my friend, I don't agree. You've just started college."

"He already told me, Rania, he said he won't interfere with my studies."

"That's what he says now, but wait until you get married and hopefully get pregnant, and then you'll see if you have the strength to continue studying. You'll fall asleep in class and run to the bathroom with nausea. You decide what you want to do. I was going to call you Hassna, to tell you that I'll come visit you next weekend so we can spend time together."

"That's great news, Rania. I'll tell Jamila to get the guest room ready."

"Hassna, I'd better put a bed in your room so we can sleep together. That way we can chat until we fall asleep."

"Okay, Rania, that's what we'll do."

Hassna couldn't sleep all night, thinking about the pros and cons that Rania had laid out for her. She wasn't sure she was making the right decision. In the early hours of the morning, she fell asleep.

Hamid arrived at his aunt and uncle's house very happy to tell them that he had asked Hassna to marry him.

"How wonderful, nephew, may Allah protect you. And what did Hassna say?"

"She was so nervous that she turned pale and I thought she was going to faint, so I suggested she give me her answer tomorrow."

"I'm thrilled, Hamid, that Omar's cousin is going to be Hassna's husband. She deserves a good man."

Hamid smiled, feeling the commitment to the loving response that was becoming increasingly urgent.

Increasingly urgent.

Latifa added, "We'll have to start preparing the marriage proposal. Your father will have to come from Morocco, and since Hassna is an orphan, she won't have a wali, so it will be a judge or Fahim who gives his consent."

"But if she gets married, she'll have to leave university," said Fahim.

"No, uncle; I promised not to interfere with her studies. She can do it in Madrid."

"You'll have to think about it very carefully, because she's a free woman, she's used to making her own decisions, and it's not easy for a man to adapt to these modern ways."

"I know, Fahim, but if I love her, we'll have to adapt to many things. I wouldn't want to lose her."

"Well, son, good luck and congratulations."

It was noon for Hassna, and Jamila was worried that her little girl was feeling ill, as she had gotten up late.

"I'll serve you breakfast or bring it to you in bed," she said to Hassna.

"Shukran Nana, I'll go to the dining room."

Hassna asked Jamila for advice. She had known her since she was a little girl and even knew what her parents would have said. After Hassna told her about Hamid's decision to marry her, Jamila asked her:

"Does my girl love him?"

Hassna replied that she did, that since her return from Morocco, not a single day had gone by without her thinking about him.

"Then what's the problem?"

"Nana, I'm afraid of going through the same thing again."

"Get that nonsense out of your head, nothing but happiness will happen, do what your heart tells you."

"Thank you, Nana." Hassna approached her and kissed her.

Hamid arrived at Hassna's house with a bouquet of flowers and a box of fine chocolates. Jamila opened the door for him, and he waited for Hassna in the living room. Jamila went to make mint tea and bring out some sweet pastries.

At the same time, Hassna entered, elegantly dressed, and found Hamid enjoying his mint tea. He stood up and greeted Hassna with a big smile, handing her the bouquet of flowers and the box of chocolates, and she accepted them, thanking him for the gesture.

"Sit down, habibati (my beloved)," he said affectionately, "how are you? Did you sleep well?"

"Yes," she replied shyly.

"Do you have an answer for me?"

"Yes, Hamid, I do, but before I answer you, I need to ask you for three conditions. First, to continue studying; second, to travel when my work requires it; and third, which is very important to me, to be your only wife.

"So, my love, will you marry me?"

"If you promise me, with your uncle as a witness, these three conditions, I will accept."

"Habibati, I will fulfill your conditions. I am crazy about you and will do everything I can to make you happy. So, habibati, let's prepare for the day of the proposal. I have to let my father know so I can travel."

Hassna seemed very happy and excited.

Hamid planned to prepare the dowry, and the bride's guardian (walli), who had to be Muslim, would be the person who, upon formalizing the marriage contract, would certify that all the written requirements had been met. If there was no walli, a judge would do so.

They had to think of three witnesses before the sheikh, an Islamic magistrate who would perform the marriage contract. After this ceremony, they would be legally and spiritually married, even if the wedding had not been celebrated, and each would return home until the date of the religious ceremony at the mosque.

Hamid thought about buying a white cotton thawb to wear to the ceremony; he would be dressed in white. Hassna would wear her Moroccan dress (takchita), along with seven other dresses.

They began to talk about the upcoming wedding and the preparations.

"I assure you, Habibati, that my aunt Latifa will be delighted to help you in any way she can to organize a beautiful wedding."

"I hope so," replied Hassna, "I won't be able to make the preparations on my own."

They said goodbye affectionately and Hamid arranged to meet her the next day.

"I'll come see you tomorrow, Habibati. It's my last day in Malaga. I have to go back to the office in Madrid and tell my father about our engagement. I assure you that everyone will be very happy that I'm finally getting married. I hope to see you again this weekend, and if I can't, maybe you can come and spend the weekend with me. We'll go for walks and you can meet my brother and his wife."

Hassna agreed to the idea.

When Hamid left to go to Fahim's house, Hassna remembered that her friend Rania was coming to visit her that weekend. She called her to tell her about the upcoming marriage proposal.

"Did you agree to marry him?"

"Yes, Rania, and you'll still be my maid of honor. I'll ask Latiffa to be the other maid of honor. This weekend we'll plan everything and go shopping for dresses for all the events. The wedding will be small. I don't have any family; Hamid has his father, his brother, and his uncles. I'm sure Latifa will help me with everything."

"Okay, friend, if you've already decided, then it's done. I'll come visit you this weekend and help you with whatever you need."

"Thank you, Rania. I knew I could count on you, as always."

The next day, Hassna went to Fahim's house as usual; Hamid had already returned to Madrid. When Latifa saw Hassna, she congratulated her on her engagement to her nephew Hamid.

"Congratulations, dear Hassna, you make a beautiful couple."

"Thank you, Latifa. I would like to ask you to help me organize the engagement and wedding and to be my maid of honor."

"Of course, Hassna, you are like our daughter. I will do it with great love. Our Omar will be delighted to have you as part of our family."

"Thank you, Latifa, I'm counting on your help."

Hamid arrived in Madrid and entered the office with a beaming face. His brother congratulated him when he found out that Hamid would no longer be single.

"Finally, brother! Who's the bride?"

"You won't believe it, her name is Hassna Sabal Saadi, she's the daughter of uncle Fahim's late partner and the ex-girlfriend and almost widow of our cousin Omar."

"What a small world. I remember the girl who was crying desperately at Omar's funeral; she was very pretty and quite young."

"I met her in the desert, saved her from dying twice, and fell in love with her from the first day I saw her."

"Does my father know? No. Even so, I have to tell him that he has to travel to Malaga for the proposal.

But, as I understand it, her parents died in a plane crash, right?"

Yes, brother.

We have to find a wali or a judge.

"When will the wedding be?"

"The proposal will be sent soon; we have to plan the wedding together. She is studying business administration at the University of Malaga; she would have to finish her degree before she could move to Madrid."

"She's a rich girl; her father was a wealthy businessman, right?"

"That's right, brother. Besides being beautiful, she's very simple and humble, although she did set some conditions."

"What?! What conditions?" Hassan was perplexed.

Hamid smiled and said, "One of them is to have only one wife, to let her continue her studies, and to let her travel if her work requires it."

Hassan laughed: "She's young and modern, brother."

"Today I'll talk to dad so he can organize his schedule and tell me when he can travel, so I can let Hassna know."

"Very good, brother, don't let it get cold. dad will be delighted to see his sister-in-law Latifa, as they haven't seen each other for a long time."

Malaga

The weekend arrived and Hassna went to pick up Rania at the airport on friday afternoon. When they saw each other, they hugged affectionately.

"Do you like my car?" Hassna asked affectionately.

"It's beautiful!" replied Rania.

"You're finally here, Rania."

"Together again, Hassna."

"That's great, my friend. I have so many things on my mind that I don't know where to start."

"First my dear Hassna, we'll make a list of the things you need for the marriage proposal."

"I don't have parents or a wali; it will be a judge who gives his consent. I need seven dresses, in addition to the wedding dress. I gave away the ones I bought for the wedding to Omar; I wouldn't wear them either. Latifa will help me find and book everything related to the food and parties."

"Okay, Hassna, that's the hardest part. I'll help you find the dresses. Let's go shopping. It's still early, so maybe we'll find something."

They arrived at an elegant shopping mall and entered a store that sold Arabic designs for elegant dresses. The store was perfumed with an incense burner, in which there were leaves wrapped and tied with a purple string placed on a small wicker circle to cleanse the air of bad vibes. They found a wide variety of dresses in beautiful colors and designs; everything she tried on fit perfectly. It was very easy and quick to find the seven dresses. The only thing missing was the wedding dress; she would have it custom made by a prestigious designer.

They returned home and Jamila welcomed them with the usual mint tea and sesame sweets, collected the purchases and placed them in Hassna's closet, then took Rania's suitcase to Hassna's bedroom, where she had prepared a place for her friend to sleep.

At that moment, Hassna's cell phone rang; it was Hamid.

"Habibati, how are you?"

"Habibi, we just got back from buying the seven dresses for the wedding. Rania is with me. She arrived this afternoon so the three of us can spend the weekend together. What time shall we pick you up?"

"Habibati, can you come to Madrid with Rania?"

"What happened? Aren't you coming?"

"I'm having a hard time getting there; I'll have to work this saturday morning. Some unexpected things have come up. Come so you can meet my brother and his wife. I'll try to finish my two meetings and when you come back, we'll go out together."

"Okay, habibi, we'll let you know when we arrive."

They packed three suitcases with clothes for the weekend and left early on saturday for Madrid.

"It'll be fun for the three of us to go out, Hassna. We can go to the Joaquín Sorolla museum," said Rania cheerfully.

"I love your idea, Rania. While Hamid finishes his work, we can go to the museum early on saturday, and then, when he's free, he can pick us up and we can have lunch together."

Hamid tried to speed up his work, and on saturday at ten in the morning, he went to pick them up at the airport.

The couple hugged each other warmly when they met. Hamid greeted Rania with a big smile and they headed for the car.

"Did you finish early, habibi?" Hassna asked him.

"Almost, habibati; I have something to do, but at noon I'll be all yours. I'll take you to my apartment. You can wait there until I'm done, and then I'll pick you up to go eat."

"Habibi, how about Rania and I visit the museum while you're busy, and when you're done, you pick us up or call me on my cell phone and we'll meet at your apartment?"

"Perfect. Enjoy Madrid, I'll be free soon."

Hamid left for his meeting. Rania and Hassna entered Hamid's beautiful apartment. It had two furnished bedrooms, a living room, a dining room, a kitchen, and a small TV room that also had a desk with a bookcase full of books on one side. In the main room, the walls displayed more works of art than a museum, and they admired the beautiful paintings. Everything in the apartment was very well decorated, modern, and tasteful. They left their luggage in the guest room and called a taxi to go to the museum.

They headed to Alcalá Street and arrived at Paseo del General Martínez Campos, where the taxi dropped them off at the door of the Sorolla Museum.

They arrived at the beautiful mansion surrounded by a lovely garden, entered the Andalusian-style house museum, and went to see the exhibition of 1,200 paintings depicting his family life, as well as ceramics and sculptures.

They toured the house museum, delighting in the gardens, which over the years had been shaded by leafy trees and surrounding buildings, leaving few plants in bloom.

They walked through the first garden, with its beautiful fountain inspired by the royal gardens of Seville, surrounded by arches and flowers. They then entered the second garden, inspired by the

170

Alhambra in Granada, decorated with predominantly blue Moorish-style tiles and a large fountain surrounded by flower pots. After touring them, they entered the second and third gardens, delighting in the sculptures and bronze reproductions that the painter later painted on canvas.

Both Rania and Hassna admired the works of Sorolla, the painter-gardener, whose works referred to his gardens and his daily life, creating a small paradise in his Spanish-Arabic Mediterranean-style gardens.

"Look, Rania, how this artist delves into contemporary painting, a realistic style, and shares some principles of impressionism by using lots of light and the absence of black."

"Rania: I love how he handles light and shadow, creating a garden to paint in his own home with familiar themes in every corner of his garden, his bucolic mansion. The truth is, I love to appreciate paintings, photos, and sketches; I imagine myself inside the canvas."

In the midst of visiting and appreciating the works of art, Rania had a mishap.

"Hassna, I need to go to the bathroom urgently."

Hassna accompanied her friend, while Rania very worried and distressed, asked Hassna to return to Hamid's apartment.

"But what's wrong? Are you feeling ill?"

"It's not that, Hassna, my period has come early and I wasn't expecting it for another three days. I haven't come prepared and I'm in a bind."

"Don't worry, let's go."

They left together and called a taxi. As they drove down General Martínez Avenue, Hassna and Rania saw Hamid smiling broadly as he left a house with a young woman who got into his car.

Hassna felt her heart freeze, as if a thousand daggers had pierced it. She couldn't believe what she was seeing. Suddenly, the blood rushed to her head and a black cloud appeared before her eyes. Her hope for a new and happy life turned to bitterness, and she once again felt hatred for the cruel fate she had been dealt. She had had a very turbulent life and felt that once again, life had changed course at this fortuitous moment. Her love crumbled into sobs and an invisible fog saturated her soul.

"Hamid, weren't you in a meeting?" Hassna said angrily. "What are you doing with that woman leaving the house?"

Hassna was enraged at the thought that Hamid was cheating on her with another woman. She thought he was wasting her time, and anger filled her broken heart. The pain she had accumulated from seeing the man of her life with a slut was a pain she did not understand how or why and her faith in him was reduced to ashes. A light went out in her face amid the rubble of disaster. This situation exacerbated her; tears welled up in her eyes. Hamid showed an unrighteous attitude, and her fate continued to weave arbitrary acts for her. She thought that the paths of this love were built on quicksand. The sky filled with black clouds that intertwined over the city. The air became sticky and it began to rain heavily, which would soon separate like drops of tears. She remembered with anger and nostalgia the feelings of past experiences and illusions. She inhaled, closing her eyes, remembering everything, every detail and place that remained, the remnants of love floating in the air, feeling completely abandoned.

"Rania, I want to go back to Malaga," Hassna said.

"First, clarify the situation; maybe it's a misunderstanding. You can't spy on and control the person you love with an iron fist. Think about it, Hassna. There must be some confusion."

"Misunderstanding! You saw the same thing I did, we're not blind. I'm not going to accept that he's dating a slut right under my nose. Listen to me carefully, I'm not going to marry a lying womanizer, nor am I going to accept his lifestyle."

The rain had stopped and a light wind had begun to blow strongly along the road. Furious, Hassna said to Rania, "This is unacceptable, it's abhorrent behavior." She stopped with a dignified and bitter gesture and said to Rania, "We're leaving. I'm not staying in this apartment a minute longer."

They arrived at Hamid's apartment, Rania changed her clothes, packed her bags, called a taxi, and they went to a hotel on Gran Via.

An hour later, Hassna's cell phone rang; it was Hamid.

"Answer it, Hassna," Rania said worriedly.

Hassna let it ring several times before picking up the phone and saying very briefly:

"Yes?"

"Habibati, what happened? I went to pick you up at the museum and you weren't there, you weren't at the apartment either, and I didn't even see your luggage. Where are you? What happened?"

"Don't you know what happened?" Hassna asked defiantly and dismissively. "Are you done with your meeting?"

"Yes, we're meeting for lunch."

"Rania had an accident at the museum and we went to your apartment. On the way, we saw you leaving a house with a woman.

Do you have meetings in private homes now? I don't want to know anything about you. Tomorrow morning we're going back to Madrid. Goodbye," and she hung up the phone.

The heated midday call exploded over Hassna, leaving her face full of rage and disappointment.

The phone rang again, but Hassna didn't answer.

Hamid didn't know where Hassna was staying; he hadn't had a chance to explain what he was doing with a woman who had left her house and got into his car. Anxiety turned to despair, and he quickened his pace to dispel it. Distressed by his own audacity, he felt a cold sweat on his hands. His blood boiled with the urgency to see her and explain the tremendous confusion; the situation weighed on him like a heavy burden. He had to rescue this poisoned situation and clear the day, so that the sky would once again be covered in deep blue.

That night, Hassna's phone rang several times, but she did not move an inch and did not answer.

Shaken by a spasmodic passion, she thought she would shed no more tears or waste her life brooding over hatred in her mind. She had already suffered a lot in her life and, like a piece of old, crumpled paper, she discarded the love she had once felt, trampling on it like wilted flowers that smelled of rotten water. She became enraged at the world and thought that Rania had been right, having rushed into love without knowing it.

Rania advised Hassna to listen to him, but she was so angry that she refused to do so.

"You're right, Rania; I shouldn't have gotten my hopes up. I was very happy on my own, and I complicated my life by falling in love."

Rania listened in silence.

They returned to Malaga in the company jet. Hamid was very hurt and worried. He had invited his brother and family for Hassna to meet them, and he feared that Hassna would break off the engagement (hotoba).

After talking to Hassan and telling him what had happened with Hassna, his brother advised him to take the first plane to Malaga to clear up the misunderstanding.

"My brother," Hassan said, "your girlfriend is very jealous, you must be very careful."

Hamid, desperate, called his aunt Latifa and told her what had happened.

"Hassna wouldn't listen to me, aunt. Help me make her understand that, after the meeting with Titrit and the notary and after signing the papers for the purchase of the property, my cousin asked me to stop by to see her, as she was near the Sorolla Museum. I thought that when we finished looking at the house, I would pick up Hassna and her friend Rania so they could meet. But when we went to pick them up, they were gone. I left my cousin at the office where she had left her car and, confused, I went to my apartment. I was surprised to find that they had left, and their luggage was gone too. I called her cell phone, and after it rang for a long time, she answered. She told me they had had an emergency and that when I returned to the apartment, they saw me leave a house with a woman and put her in the car. I didn't have time to say anything to her; after that, she never answered my calls. I don't know where they are.

"Calm down, Hamid, I'll find out what happened and where she is."

While Hamid ran after her like an antelope, taking the first flight to Malaga, his aunt Latifa would take care of calming everyone down by the time he arrived.

Malaga

The girls arrived in Malaga and went to pick up Hassna's car from the garage next to the airport hangar. They headed home. When she opened the door, Jamila was surprised at how quickly she had returned. Hassna told her nanny what had happened. She shook her head disapprovingly at Hamid's behavior. She went to the kitchen and brought linden tea for her little girl and mint tea for Rania, with sesame sweets.

It was getting dark and Latifa came to visit. Jamila opened the door and let her in.

"Salam aleikum, ma'am."

"Alaikum assalam," replied Latifa.

"Please sit down; I'll call my little girl, ma'am."

Jamila went to call Hassna, who was in her bedroom with Rania. She came out of the bedroom and walked into the living room with a grim expression. Latifa saw a dangerous glint in her eyes, revealing a torrent of disturbing doubts.

They hugged, and Hassna burst into tears.

"You don't know what happened," she said to Latifa with a broken heart. "We talked about this before we got engaged, and he didn't respect it."

"I know, my dear daughter," said her aunt.

"Did he send you to ask me to forgive him?" Hassna asked.

Latifa took Hassna's hands and explained, "Hassna, that girl you saw is our niece Titrit, my younger sister's daughter. When Hamid's mother fell ill, Titrit cared for her lovingly until the day she died; she and Hamid are first cousins. She is married and has two young children."

Hassna, fully recovered and thinking more calmly, fell silent, regretting her jealous outburst, and asked Latifa:

"How do you know it's the same person I saw with him?"

Latifa had a photo ready.

"Is this the person you saw with Hamid?"

Hassna looked at it and nodded.

"You see, dear, it was a misunderstanding. Hamid came to Malaga to see you and clear everything up. He's out there."

Hamid stood nervously, as straight as a lit cigarette between his fingers, waiting for Hassna to be convinced of the misunderstanding.

Hassna sent Jamila to let him in.

When they met, they embraced, and Hassna fell into his arms, ashamed of the tantrum she had thrown.

"Forgive me, Hamid," said Hassna, "I shouldn't have judged you so lightly. I should have let you speak, but jealousy and anger got the better of me."

"It's okay, habibati, it's all forgotten," he said as he hugged her, feeling a burning sensation in his chest.

Once reconciled, their love grew stronger. They had to trust each other and continued with the preparations for the marriage proposal.

Latifa had everything ready; she suggested to Hassna that Fahim be her wali, since he had known her since she was a child. She gladly accepted.

"Thank you, Latifa. Fahim is like a father to me," Hassna replied.

The day of the hotoba arrived, and Hamid attended the ceremony with his father.

Hassna appeared dressed in a beautiful beige caftan embroidered with gold. She looked truly beautiful, with a hijab covering her hair.

That afternoon, everything was ready for the dowry to be presented, a gift that the groom prepared for the bride. In this case, Hamid gave her a beautiful two-carat diamond ring set in gold as part of the dowry.

The Walli was Fahim, as the bride's guardian; he would ensure that all the stipulations written in the contract were fulfilled.

At the beginning of the ceremony, Fahim and the groom shook hands in greeting, and the sheikh spoke about the importance of marriage. He read the suras on how the bride and groom should behave. He then asked Hassna if she wanted to marry Hamid, and vice versa. Both accepted. The opening sura of the Quran, Al-Fatiha, was recited, and they were officially married.

They had refreshments and exchanged milk and dates between the bride and groom. The milk symbolized purity and the dates symbolized prosperity.

After the ceremony, Hassna and Hamid were married, but each would have to return home until the wedding day at the mosque. There were many congratulations and good wishes for the bride and groom. Rania looked sad; her friend was moving away from her; she would never be the same again.

The bride and groom presented three witnesses before the Islamic magistrate (sheikh). The witnesses were Rania, Hassan, Hamid's brother, and Latifa, who signed the marriage contract. After this ceremony, the bride and groom were legally and spiritually united, even though the religious ceremony had not yet been held.

After the ceremony, the bride and groom returned to their respective homes to plan the wedding celebration at the mosque and the date on which it would take place.

The day after the Hotoba, Hassna and Hamid met for a family lunch at Latifa's house. Hamid's brother and his wife were there, as well as his father, Habbib, who had traveled from Morocco to attend the engagement. Rania was also present at the family lunch.

Hamid announced that the religious wedding would take place in a month's time, which gave them time to prepare for the ceremony. Everyone was very happy and shared a delicious Moroccan-style lunch. Hamid's father chatted at length with Hassna, telling her that he had met her parents and was delighted that she was the girl who had gotten lost in the desert and that Hamid had turned the desert upside down to find her. Everyone smiled.

After the invitation, Rania and Hassna went home. Hassna was exhausted after those two intense days and had to prepare for her religious wedding in a month.

Hassna noticed that Rania was different, a little upset or angry. She didn't know what was wrong, and when she asked, Rania replied.

"I don't think you did the right thing by getting engaged so soon without knowing each other. I hope it works out for you and that you don't regret it."

Hassna didn't respond and continued doing her thing. Rania had come to Malaga for the hotoba ceremony and had to return to Granada to attend university.

They said goodbye with the intention of seeing each other the following weekend to accompany Hassna to her wedding dress fitting.

Latifa took charge of the preparations for the reception at the mosque, including the invitations, flowers, food, and decorations. She was as excited as if it were Omar who was getting married.

A month before the wedding, Hassna's wedding dress was being made by a renowned Arab designer. The religious wedding would be held in a mosque and the reception would take place in the gardens of Fahim's residence, which was a very suitable venue for the event.

During the week, Rania insisted on the phone that she shouldn't get married so soon. Hassna began to doubt whether it was a good idea to get married so hastily. Perhaps Rania was right to wait about six months, Hassna thought, although Jamila encouraged her to follow her heart.

Hassna continued to make preparations with Latifa with great enthusiasm and spoke daily with Hamid, who was falling more and more in love with her every day and was eager to have her by his side.

The weekend arrived and Hassna picked up Rania from the airport and accompanied her to her wedding dress fitting.

Hassna looked so beautiful she resembled an Arabian queen. The dress hardly needed any alterations; it was practically perfect. Hassna was radiant with happiness in her white dress embroidered with rhinestones, matching the veil sprinkled with tiny Swarovski crystal beads.

After the fitting, Rania asked Hassna to drive the car and park it while Hassna went down to the florist to order and choose the flowers for her wedding bouquet. Hassna agreed.

As Hassna crossed the street, Rania was distracted and while looking at the florist's, a truck ran a red light and drove straight ahead, hitting the convertible on the driver's side. The small car's left side was destroyed, caved in, crushing Rania's body.

Hassna tried to help her friend, shouting,

"Help! Call an ambulance!"

Rania, badly injured, with broken bones and a ruptured spleen, gasped in a broken voice and said a few words to her friend who was holding her head from outside the car.

"Hassna, forgive me, I was selfish. Hamid is a good man, marry him. I was jealous because I have always loved you and wanted you all to myself, and since you are my friend, I was happy to have you close by. I never showed you my feelings because I knew you were different from me."

"Rania, please don't talk. You'll be fine, my friend. Hang in there."

"I love you, Hassna."

Hassna cried, trying to wake Rania, who was fainting. The paramedics took her away in the ambulance, and when she arrived at the hospital, there was nothing they could do; Rania had passed away.

Hassna, upon learning that her sister had died, burst into tears.

Latifa received a call from the hospital and rushed over with Fahim to take care of Hassna. They notified Rania's father, who was in Granada, to give him the sad news.

Hamid learned from Fahim what had happened and flew to Malaga to comfort Hassna over the loss of her best friend.

Hamid's uncles took Hassna home, where she was seen by a doctor and prescribed painkillers to ease the shock of the accident.

Rania's father arranged for his daughter to be taken to a funeral home as soon as possible so that the body could be prepared according to Arab-Muslim customs and the funeral could be organized within three days of her death, while he made his way to the city of Malaga.

Hamid arrived at Fahim's house. Hassna was asleep. He entered the room, took her hand, and said:

"May Allah continue to protect you, Habibati. I don't know what I would have done if something had happened to you." He kissed her hand and stayed with her.

When the effect of the painkillers wore off, Hassna asked about Rania, where she was and if her father had been told.

Latifa replied that he was taking care of everything related to the funeral.

Hamid stayed with Hassna the whole time, even during the wake.

Hassna was deeply saddened by the death of her only friend, who was almost like a sister to her, and she kept the secret that Rania had revealed to her before she died. Hassna never told anyone so that her friend would not be judged. She thought that Rania had saved her life again, this time by asking for the steering wheel while she was going to the florist to order her flowers.

A month later, the wedding date was set and preparations began for the three days during which Hassna would prepare for marriage.

The first day was a symbolic purification, the beginning of a new stage for women. They visited a public bathhouse where she took a steam bath to relieve stress for seven consecutive nights in the company of her friends. She was accompanied by Latifa, Hassan's wife, and some of Hamid's cousins. Hassna missed her inseparable friend Rania.

They were served juices and given foot massages with argan, rose, and sandalwood oil. It was like her bachelorette party: they formed a procession with dancing, incense, singing, a jacuzzi, and aromatherapy. Afterwards, they took a limousine ride with dinner and a show.

On the second day, the protection ritual was performed; a professional applied henna tattoos to her hands and feet, with passages from the Quran engraved on them, along with floral and geometric designs, as protection against the evil eye.

After all these events, a family meal was held.

Hamid met with his friends and family, all of whom were men. Hassna met separately with her female friends and family at a house and a restaurant. The men danced with open arms to Arabic music and lifted Hamid up, applauding and shouting, "Long live the groom!"

Hamid swore allegiance to his friends, performing the ritual to bring good luck to the marriage and make it last forever.

The men's party was generally very boring; they read some verses from the Koran, had dinner, and chatted, unlike the women's party, which was more fun.

On the third day, the wedding celebration took place at Fahim and Latifa's house. A large, illuminated tent had been set up in the garden, beautifully decorated with expensive Arabian rugs and brightly colored cushions, ornate round tables, and large golden lamps that illuminated the tables with a soft light.

While waiting for Hassna, her friends and family drank milk and ate dates, beginning the ceremony seated on comfortable cushions until Hassna appeared in her wedding dress, accompanied by music. She was brought in a beautiful, radiant carriage, and the magic of her dream had come true. Her friends and family carried her, dressed dazzlingly like an Arab princess, with makeup and a beautiful hairstyle under her veil, and a bouquet of white roses in her hands. She was accompanied by Arabic shouts (zaghareet), moving their tongues from right to left, emitting a high-pitched tone that her friends cheered as she entered. Hassna stood in the center, covered with a red veil, while her friends continued to sing and spin around her.

The food served, as usual, reflected the family's wealth. The banquet menu was carefully prepared and offered tasty dishes, from pasta to seafood. Sultan's salad: eggplant, peppers, olives, and Manchego cheese. Chicken pie with puff pastry, drizzled with honey and sauce, lamb, chicken tagine with lemon, olives, and couscous. Beef or chicken stew with vegetables. A variety of breads, mint tea, and sugar. On a special table, there were Moroccan Arabic wedding cookies and delicious sweets.

Hamid, the celebration ended soon, announced that he was arriving with his guests to join the women. They covered their heads with abayas to welcome Hamid and his companions. Hassna looked beautiful dressed in white, and her friends accompanied her with lit candles.

When Hamid entered the celebration, he was also dressed in white with a floor-length thawb. The women sat in armchairs next to Hassna and toasted with Sharbat, a non-alcoholic drink made with rose water, oranges, or apples.

Hamid and Hassna presided over the ceremony from a central chair, looking regal, full of light and hope. Depending on the occasion, Hassna glided with the grace of a gazelle and changed several times as necessary into beautiful dresses of various colors embroidered with gold and silver thread.

The bride and groom lovingly exchanged rings from their right hands to their left index fingers, thus concluding the ritual. They looked at each other with tenderness and overflowing love, confident that no dark cloud would ever overshadow the union of their dreams.

After the wedding, Hamid took Hassna to the best hotel in Malaga to consummate the marriage. As Hamid's house was in Madrid, his friends kidnapped Hassna and took her away in a palanquin, celebrating with great fanfare until they left her in the hotel's bridal suite.

Latifa, representing Hamid's mother, presented Hassna with a tray of milk and dates as a sign of welcome, and gave her a set of keys and a loaf of bread as a way of offering her a new home.

"The milk will bring purity to your life, Hassna, and the dates are a symbol of fortune and abundance," said Latifa. Hassna thanked her with a beautiful smile.

When Hamid crossed the threshold of the bedroom door, he recited verses from the Quran in front of Hassna, removed the veil covering her beautiful face, and kissed her forehead gently. Hassna was happy, but at the same time tense as the strings of a violin. When Hamid approached her, her muscles relaxed until she surrendered herself into the arms of her beloved, transforming that night into a dance of stars so joyful that they could reach the sky.

Hamid gently undressed Hassna until she lay naked on his bed. He covered her with kisses and passion. Hassna's dream came true, sailing into a peaceful dream of a satisfied woman ; she was completely happy. For many hours, they disappeared from the world, savoring every inch of her skin with infinite patience and tenderness. Hamid was the man of her life, and they wrapped themselves in the veil of Hamid's passion, making her his. Then they reinvented love, exhausted and bathed in sweat. The sheet was stained by the loss of her virginity, which Hamid would protect to show to the family that awaited her.

Once the marriage was consummated, both spouses and lovers enjoyed exploring each other's bodies and feeling different sensations of love, hoping that Allah would bless them with numerous descendants.

They spent three days at the hotel enjoying their honeymoon. Then, the radiant couple said goodbye to Latifa and Fahim before embarking on their journey home.

Jamila stayed in the house until her young girl and husband arrived in Malaga to visit her.

They arrived in Madrid and walked under the shade of the trees until they entered the apartment. Hamid carried his beloved wife in his arms to their new home, enjoying a beautiful sunset. Hassna felt fulfilled and happy to finally share her life with the man she loved. Early in the morning, they left on their honeymoon to the desert, where Hamid offered her his love, comparable to that immense desert, while the midday light reflected in Hassna's black, almond-shaped eyes. They rode for long hours on dromedaries through the golden sands of the Sahara, where kisses and caresses melted softly into the moonlight, remembering the place where they met and waited there, in a tent, until she became pregnant, according to Arab-Muslim tradition, turning the Sahara into a "desert of love."

Upon her return to Madrid, Hassna took charge of the head office, continued her studies at university, and became a perfect wife and mother, as well as an excellent executive.

End.

BIOGRAPHY

Mariangela Delfino Cavero is one of the most promising new writers of modern Peruvian fiction.

Born in Lima, Peru, she is a US citizen. She studied at the Sagrado Corazón School in Lima, Peru.

She took courses in painting and drawing at the Art Center Lima-Peru.

She also studied at Miami Dade Community College and has worked as a Spanish teacher in the United States for twelve years.

Her tireless wanderlust has taken her to various corners of the globe, including North, Central, and South America, Europe, Asia, and Africa, with the aim of capturing the history, customs, and knowledge of the places she has visited in her novels, encouraging her readers to visit them and those who have already visited them to remember them.

She currently lives in Venice, Florida.

She has written other novels:

English:

Legacy from Beyond, 2026

Spanish edition:

Deje todo por Amor 2018

Atrapadas en la Oscuridad, 2019

El Purgatorio de los inocentes 2011